The Alpha Plague

Michael Robertson

Website and Newsletter:
www.michaelrobertson.co.uk

Email: subscribers@michaelrobertson.co.uk

Edited by:
Aaron Sikes, Terri King, And
Sara Jones

Cover Design by Dusty Crosley

Formatting by Polgarus Studio

The Alpha Plague
Michael Robertson
© 2015 Michael Robertson

In the Name of Science started life as a five thousand–word short story. It kick-started my writing career when it was accepted by HarperCollins to appear in the back of their eBook version of Laurence Obrian's *The Jerusalem Puzzle*. Having this work accepted gave me the confidence to put more of my writing out in the world.

Since writing this story, I've often wanted to come back to it. I renamed it *The Alpha Plague: Genesis* because, although it started as a short story, I soon realised that it's actually the beginning of a series of novels—book two is currently being edited.

The book you have now is the first book growing out of my original short. If you've already read the short, you'll find it interspersed through the first few chapters in this book. If you haven't, there's no need, this book stands on its own.

Thank you for buying my book and I hope you like it.

Michael Robertson
June 2015

Chapter One

Alice pressed her fork down on her steak. The soft meat leaked a pool of blood that spread over her white plate. It soaked into the potatoes and broccoli.

A slow heave lifted in her throat, and she gulped several times to combat the excess saliva that gushed into her mouth. She could almost taste the metallic tang of blood. "How was the—" another heave rose up and she cleared it with a cough that echoed through the sparse room. She tried again. "How was the lab today, John?"

A thick frown furrowed John's brow. This was his usual response to most questions. Everything was an irritation. Such banal conversations couldn't hold a flame to his vast intellect. He ejected the word as if giving a reply was below him. "Stressful."

The rejection sent a sharp stab through Alice's stomach. It didn't matter how many times he knocked her down, she got back up and continued to look for his approval. Fire spread beneath her cheeks and she chewed on her bottom lip.

John flashed a grin of wonky teeth. It took all of Alice's strength not to flinch at the ghastly sight. "I must say though, it's been made a little easier by Wilfred having to make me this meal."

A deep breath filled Alice's sinuses with the smell of disinfectant; the smell she associated with John. Decades immersed in the study of bacteria and disease had driven his level of cleanliness to the point where it bordered on obsessive-compulsive. A frown darkened her view of the room. "What did you say the bet was?"

"I didn't."

Alice looked into his sharp blue eyes and waited for him to say more.

He didn't.

A look first at the man, dressed in his white lab coat, she then looked around at his white, minimalist penthouse apartment. Everything had a place, and everything was necessary. Beakers and test tubes littered the sides like ornaments. She hadn't ever seen a photograph on display, despite this being his personal space… no room for sentimentality here.

Alice squirmed in her seat as the silence swelled.

John watched her.

No matter how long she'd known the man for, John always made her itch in her own skin. As if pressured to break the overwhelming void between them, she said, "So, what was the bet about?"

"An experiment. I predicted the correct result."

A machine would have been better company. Alice frowned at him again and sighed.

"Oh, do pull yourself together, woman," John said. "You've got to learn to stop being so bloody sensitive."

Despite his obnoxious behaviour, the man did have redeeming qualities. When he worked, his creativity and passion flowed from him. Science drove him like a heartbeat, but Alice couldn't excuse *him time and again. She couldn't ignore every time he'd humiliated her during a lecture; every time he'd not let her finish her point; every time he'd selected her to clean the lab at the end of the day while he let his other students leave. "How about you learn to stop being so bloody **in**sensitive?"*

A flick of his bony hand at her and he said, "This is what I mean. It's these emotional fluctuations that take away your ability to be objective. That's why men make better scientists."

"And terrible companions."

He lowered his head and peered over his glasses at her. "We can leave our baggage at the door," he continued.

For the second time, her face smouldered. "You left your baggage in the delivery ward, John. Maybe your sociopathic detachment serves you well in the world of science, but it doesn't equip you to deal with the real world. Without science, you'd be stranded." Her vision blurred. Great! Tears again. They only strengthened the man's argument.

John sighed and shook his head.

A glance down at her dinner, and Alice prodded the soft steak. Maybe a scalpel would be more appropriate than the wooden-handled knife in her hand. In the bright glare of John's scrutiny, Alice cut into the steak and lifted a piece to her mouth.

The soft meat sat like jelly on her tongue. Unable to chew it, she took a deep gulp and tried to swallow. The piece of steak stuck in her throat like it was barbed. Her heart raced as a metallic rush of juices slithered down her oesophagus and clogged her throat.

John watched on, his expression unchanged. The cold detachment of a scientist rather than the compassion of a human being stared through his beady eyes.

Alice's pulse boomed inside her skull. She held her neck and wheezed, "Help me."

He didn't. He believed in natural selection. Sink or swim. How many cavemen had choked on their dinner? The ones who had been saved only weakened the gene pool. Weakness should never be rewarded.

After several heavy gulps, Alice swallowed the meat, leaned on the table, and gasped. Adrenaline surged through her. Her pulse pounded in her ears. She dabbed her eyes with the back of her hand to stop her mascara from running and looked up to see John watching her with his usual blank expression. A barrage of abuse rose and died on her tongue; there was no point.

Alice retuned her focus to her dinner and flinched every time her cutlery hit the porcelain plate. The sharp chinks bounced around the quiet room. After she'd cut everything up, she stared at her food. A tightness remained in her throat from when she'd choked; another sip of warm red wine did little to ease her trepidation.

When she looked back up, John still watched her.

She cleared her throat. "So, when will you tell me about your work, John?"

His dinner remained untouched; his scrawny frame and pallid skin served as a visual representation of his poor diet. Thirty years her senior at sixty-three, he looked fifty years older. He consulted his wristwatch as if their meal had a deadline and sighed. "I can't. You know that."

While she watched him, she speared some potato and put it in her mouth, chewed, and took another sip of wine. The fluffy vegetable disintegrated and slid down her throat when she swallowed. Eating under John's cold scrutiny seemed to increase the possibility that she'd choke again. Maybe he was right; maybe her tension was all in the mind.

She ate a piece of purple sprouting broccoli. The bland vegetable had taken on the rich tang of blood from the steak.

Despite the slow heave that turned through her stomach again, Alice focused hard on mastication. When the food had no taste left, she swallowed the weak mush.

When she looked up again, the strip lighting sent electric shocks through her eyeballs. She shielded her brow as she looked at John. "Have the lights gotten brighter?"

John didn't respond.

"The lights," she repeated as she viewed the room through slits. "Have they been turned up?" Her world blurred, and the beginnings of a migraine stretched its poisonous roots through her brain.

Alice changed the subject. "I know you can't tell me about your work, John. It's just, as my professor, I long to understand more. You're here to teach me, after all." Another sharp pain jabbed into her eyes, and she drew a short breath that echoed in the bare room. While she stared down at the white table, she pinched her forehead for relief.

"Are you okay?" His tone showed no evidence of concern. It seemed more like someone on a scientific quest to collate information. She expected to look up and see him taking notes. John didn't believe in downtime. The world should be viewed through objective eyes at all times. Emotions belonged to the irrational.

Two hollow knocks sounded out when John dropped his pointy elbows on the table. Alice looked up to see his long and bony fingers entwine. His deep and languid voice rumbled, "Eat more, it will make you feel better. As for my work, you'll have to keep wondering,

I'm afraid. Since the Second Cold War started with The East, everything has been on a need-to-know basis."

"The Second Cold War? That's always your excuse, John. Since the terrorist attacks in 2023—"

"And the second wave a year later." He spoke to her as if she didn't know her history. He spoke to her as if she barely knew her own name.

A deep breath helped her withhold her retort. "The point I was trying to make," she said, "is that nothing's happened for the last fifteen years. We've had the silent threat of war hanging over us like a thick fog. Sometimes I wonder whether it's just a way for the government to take our civil liberties away. I wouldn't be surprised if they put a Doomsday Clock in every city just to remind us of how much protection we need. Just so we obey their every wish."

"Don't be ridiculous, Alice. You sound like one of those new-age paranoid types."

"As opposed to the old-age paranoid types? At least my beliefs don't result in us stockpiling weapons of mass destruction." Fire spread across her face and she trembled. Years of repressed arguments always rushed forward when things got tense between them. One day he'd get the lot, regardless of whether he labelled her irrational or not.

His long features twisted, but he remained silent.

"Besides, when you're connected to those in power, I'm sure it does seem preposterous. You'll be okay, John; you have a space in their fallout shelters when you want it. Ironic really."

"What is?"

She gasped when her stomach lurched. She coughed several times before she said, "The fact that the wealthy and privileged will

THE ALPHA PLAGUE

survive if it all goes to hell, left to remake the world in their own greedy image. I mean,"—she forced a laugh that fell dead in the sparse room—"that's what got us in this state in the first place. It would seem that humanity is destined to repeat itself if they're the people who will crawl out of the ground after this planet has been ravaged by a nuclear war." A huge gulp of wine, and she slammed the glass back down on the table. When she pulled her hair from her face, the light in the room hit her like sharp needles fired into her eyeballs.

A gentle slur dampened her words, and the warm liquid that she'd tried to drink dribbled down her chin. "Anyway, maybe we'll work together when I graduate."

When she looked back up, she saw regret in his cold eyes. The flicker of emotion sat awkwardly on his stony face. "Maybe," he allowed. "How's your food? Wilfred is quite the chef, don't you think?"

If Wilfred never cooked again it would be too soon. Alice didn't reply.

John maintained the silence.

No matter how much she wriggled, Alice found no comfort on the hard plastic chair. Sweat dampened her back. Before she spoke, she paused. The words had abandoned her, so she fished in her increasingly foggy mind for them. The first three words came out as a slur, "Yes, he is. However, the steak is a little rare for my liking." A hard throb surged through her temples. She drew a sharp breath through her clenched teeth and slapped her hands to her face. When she pushed against her eyeballs, it did nothing to ease her pain; they felt ready to burst.

John showed little concern. After he'd regarded his watch again, he lifted a small black box and pressed a button on it. "I agree. Wilfred likes his meat bloody." He said the word like a vampire with a thirst. "This is well done by his standards."

A gentle whir sounded, and darkness fell over the room.

When Alice twisted her head, she saw heavy metal shutters close over the windows. "When were they fitted?" she asked. Her own words echoed through her mind.

A half smile twisted John's face. "Earlier today."

Every beat of her pulse kicked her brain. Her stomach tensed. She stammered, "W... why are you... um, why are you locking us in?"

His laugh echoed through her skull and her world spun. "I'm not locking us in, dear. I'm locking them out. We've had information that suggests the Cold War may heat up tonight. We believe that China and Korea have mastered biological warfare. This apartment is already well fortified; I've just added the shutters to prevent an airborne virus from entering." As if in afterthought, he added, "I'm sure that nothing will happen, but it's better to be safe."

Fire barrelled through her guts. Sweat gushed from her brow, and the thick black bars of tunnel vision shut off her peripheral sight. Everything fell into soft focus. She felt disconnected from the words as she said them. "Oh, so we have to stay here?" Several blinks did nothing to clear her vision.

With a sombre nod, John said, "Yes. We have plenty of rations though."

Where? The apartment had seemed empty—not that she could see much now; maybe she'd missed a stash of supplies.

Another rush of heat forced sweat from every pore. John vanished *from her view as his white coat blended into the surroundings.*

Alice wheezed. "Is that why you're checking your watch? You know when it's supposed to happen?"

Before John replied, everything went dark and she fell sideways. Sharp pain exploded across her cheek as she hit the table. The smell of bleach slithered up her nostrils.

"It won't be long now, dear."

She heard his chair scrape across the floor.

"Would you excuse me while I go and use the bathroom? I want to make the most of that luxury because we'll need to stay in this room from here on out. It'll be a bucket in the corner after thisssssssssss..."

His words faded as her vision failed her.

***

The sun shone directly into Rhys' eyes when he pulled up outside Dave's house. On the first attempt, he flapped at the sun visor and missed it, the glare so strong it blinded him. The thing creaked when he flipped it down on the second attempt. The car was a relic, but it wasn't like he could afford anything else. When the custody battle for his boy was finally over with, he'd get one of the latest models. The Audi Aurore had automatic sun visors as standard from the 2035 model onwards. It may be a few years old, but something like that would be much nicer than the twenty-year-old Peugeot piece of shit he had to drive.

He left the engine running to keep the air conditioner on. Dave wouldn't be out straight away, and Rhys refused to cook in the car while he waited.

Nauseous dread sat in Rhys' stomach as it did every Monday

morning. As clichéd as it was to hate Mondays, Rhys couldn't fucking stand them. They served as a sharp reminder that another weekend had passed where he hadn't seen his son.

A quick toot of the horn, and he leaned back in his seat to wait.

***

Rhys checked his watch for the sixth time, at least; a minute had passed, maybe more. The cool air blew on Rhys' face. It stung his eyes slightly as the prolonged jet dried them out while he stared at Dave's blue front door. Rhys expected him to be late, but he'd usually acknowledged Rhys' presence by now. Dishevelled hair and bleary eyes would have normally poked their head out of the door and winced the usual apology of the perpetually late, but he got nothing today.

Another check of his watch, and Rhys tooted the horn again.

Dave 'ten more minutes' Allen always needed ten more minutes. They now had an agreement in place; Dave could have ten more minutes, but once that time had elapsed, Rhys left for work with or without him. At thirty-five, Dave could take responsibility for getting himself to work on time. Rhys often felt like his fucking mother.

***

Seven minutes left of the ten and still no sign of Dave. The corners of Rhys' eyes itched as he continued to watch Dave's front door. A quick check in the rear-view mirror, and he saw his own scowl. No wonder his eyes ached. Maybe he should just go now. Sod ten minutes. Dave can find his own damn way to work.

A heavy sigh, and Rhys shook his head. He couldn't do that, no matter how much he wanted to... not with their agreement in place. He reached up to press the horn again, but before he had the chance to, a loud *bang* crashed into the window next to him.

Rhys' heart leaped into his throat and he spun around to find himself face to face with the messy-haired Dave. His afro looked like a bird's nest. "What the fuck, man?" Not that he needed to ask; the stubble and bloodshot eyes told Rhys exactly what Dave had been up to. When he wound the window down, the heat of the morning rushed into the car with the reek of stale booze. Surprise, surprise.

"I'm sorry, mate," Dave said.

Rhys looked past Dave at the house he'd just left. Like Dave's house, it provided affordable living for the young professional. "You fucked Julie again?"

A half smile, and Dave shrugged. "How long have I got before you leave?"

After a glance down at the dash, Rhys said, "Four minutes." He had six, but Dave always needed the wiggle room.

Without another word, Dave jogged toward his house. A sprint would have no doubt reproduced most of the consumed alcohol from the previous night, and Rhys didn't need to see that, even if it did mean Dave moved slower.

The electric window whirred as Rhys did it up again, and the leather seat groaned when he leaned back into it. Despite the cool air conditioning, the heat of the sun warmed his face, and he closed his eyes. One day, Dave would surprise him by being on time.

Yeah, right.

***

When Dave opened the car door, Rhys opened his eyes again. A glance at the clock, and he quickly sat upright. The cheeky fucker had taken twelve minutes from him; it best not fuck things up for seeing his boy. The opportunities for him to see Flynn were few and far between. The last thing he needed was Dave ruining that, even though he couldn't ever know what time to pass Flynn's school because his mother was so damn inconsistent. When they'd been together, Larissa kept time like an army sergeant. Now she turned up whenever she fucking liked. She used it as a way to fuck with him, a way of repeated punishment for his one mistake.

"Sorry again, mate," Dave said as he strapped his seatbelt on. "I don't have my alarm at Julie's."

Rhys made a quick check over his shoulder and signalled before he pulled away. Being pissed with him wouldn't help, but Rhys couldn't let go of the tension that gripped his jaw. Not that he could really blame Dave; he could have left him after ten minutes like they'd previously agreed.

A deep sigh, and Rhys rolled his shoulders. It loosened the tension slightly. "What's going on with you two? That's the fifth time in the past fortnight that you've stayed over there."

"You know what it's like, mate; we go out on the piss, bump into each other all drunk and horny, one thing leads to another…"

"Why don't you just start dating her? You're thirty-five now, Dave, you ain't getting any younger."

"Exactly."

Rhys raised an eyebrow at him. "Huh?"

"I have less time left in my life," Dave explained. "Do you seriously think I need to fill what's left of whatever existence I have with the bullshit of being attached to somebody? I like fucking; I don't like going to garden centres on a Sunday and picking out potted plants. Besides, you're hardly a shining example to follow when it comes to relationships."

"That was below the belt, mate."

"Tell me I'm wrong."

Rhys shook his head. "Whatever."

"Do you remember when you were out on the weekends with us? The wild nights on the town with the boys?"

Of course he remembered them. The hint of a smile lifted his lips.

Despite his apparent lethargy, Dave jumped on it. "See? They were fun times... bullshit chat up lines that worked more often than not, a different woman every night, dancing until the early hours, and a takeaway on the way home. When you wake up in a strange bed with a naked woman and a half-eaten kebab in your pocket, you knew you'd had a good night. How's that not fun?"

When they rounded the next bend, the sun shone directly into the front of the car. The glare burned Rhys' eyes, but it seemed like nothing compared to Dave. First he shrieked, hid behind his forearms, and then flapped around until he'd found his sunglasses and slipped them on.

"What are you," Rhys said, "a fucking vampire?"

"The hangovers get harder with each passing week, man. I'm getting too old for this."

"Yeah, I don't miss that."

"You should come out with us one weekend. I know the boys would be pleased to see you."

"I would," Rhys said, "but I have different priorities now. I'm a dad and I need to behave like one. I may have troubles with Larissa, but Flynn is my reason for being. I need to do the right thing by him."

The route to work always passed Flynn's school. Of course, Rhys wanted to arrive at work on time, but he lived for the chance to pass Flynn when he got dropped off at the gates. Just one glance of his little boy could keep him going for a week or more.

When they got close, Rhys slowed down and looked across at all the children. Dave shut up as Rhys continued to search. Between eight and nine, all of the kids got dropped off by their parents; a quick glance at the clock on the dash showed him it was eight twenty-three.

***

Even after they'd passed the primary school, Rhys continued to look over his shoulder. Not that it served any purpose; there were only a handful of kids, and most of them were girls.

As Rhys sped up, Dave rubbed his temples and reclined into his seat again. "No Flynn today?"

Did it look like Flynn was there today? Rhys pushed out a heavy sigh to try to force some of his frustration away. "No, I swear she drops him at a different time every day just to fuck with me. All I want is a small glance of him, a wave before I go to work. I just want him to know how much I love him. I don't want him to forget me. Instead, I feel like a fucking stalker… a nonce that slows down and stares at the children going into school." With his jaw clenched, he added, "I swear she gets some sick pleasure from it."

It may have been a clumsy hand, guided by an exhausted and clearly still intoxicated man, but when Dave squeezed Rhys' shoulder, it sent a shimmer of sadness through his heart. The sting of tears itched his eyeballs, and he continued to stare straight ahead.

"He won't forget you, mate. Six year olds know who their parents are, even if they're separated. When did you see him last?"

"About a week and a half ago."

"So Saturday's your next day with him?"

With a grip so tight on the wheel it hurt his hands, Rhys' breathed quicker. "That's the plan. If she doesn't fucking cancel, that is."

"She's still cancelling a lot?"

"Yeah, whenever she damn well feels like it."

Dave let go of Rhys' shoulder, leaned back, and shook his head. "What a bitch."

Rhys didn't reply.

Chapter Two

He may have been dressed in the same sterile uniform as his colleague—a full-length lab coat, white trousers, and black shoes—but Wilfred liked to think the similarities ended there. He and John belonged to different planets. Hell, they belonged to different galaxies. Just the sight of the tall and skinny man curdled his guts.

He ran a hand through his hair and asked, "Is she okay?"

A leer cracked John's angular face as he stood on the other side of the door to his lab and stared in through the window. "No, I don't think she is." When he looked at his colleague, his piercing blue eyes shone bright in his craggy face. "But that's the point, isn't it?"

A cold chill ran the length of Wilfred's body as a violent, yet concise, shiver. His hands balled into fists as he looked at the wrinkly man in front of him. If he drove John's face hard enough into the door, he could smash his beak of a nose. Let's see what happened to his cold detachment then. After he'd cleared his throat, Wilfred said, "How was the meal?"

Excitement lit John's features; he hadn't been this animated in years. "It went well." He then turned back to the window.

A deep frown, and Wilfred spoke slow and deliberate words. He had to hold onto his fury. His moment would come. "I didn't make the meal, so why did you tell her I did?"

"Isn't it obvious?" John laughed. "She wouldn't have believed I'd made it. I didn't want her to be suspicious." He lifted an eyebrow and added, "We needed her to eat it, after all."

Reluctant to look into the room, Wilfred kept his attention on John. "And she ate the steak? It wasn't too bloody?"

"It was, but it had to be; we couldn't cook the virus."

Heat radiated from Wilfred's cheeks. Why had John done it?

A few seconds of silence passed before John turned to his colleague. "What's wrong with you? Are you letting your emotions get the better of you again?"

Wilfred ground his jaw and counted silently to three. He took a deep breath, exhaled, and moved next to the skinny man. When he got close enough, the taste of bleach hit the back of his throat. John smelled like a swimming pool. No matter how much time Wilfred spent around the man, he'd never get used to it. He then looked through the window.

A rich kick of bile rose in Wilfred's throat when he saw Alice slumped over the table in the middle of the room. Pain tore through his chest to look at her blonde hair splayed out like a halo. What had she done to deserve this?

"It happened exactly like the dogs we tested it on, Wilfred. The blood vessels in her eyes exploded and turned the whites red in an instant. They even bled." A huge grin opened up John's long face, and his eyes spread wide. "I could predict exactly when to leave. Exactly!"

Unable to look away from the woman in the room, Wilfred

jumped when she twitched. The surge of adrenaline ran a gentle shake through his hands. It was different to see it happen to dogs— he didn't have a relationship with them like he had with Alice. A lump rose in his throat, and he swallowed against it. "Is she okay?"

"Of course she's not okay. That's the point!"

Of course. Stupid bloody question.

Another glance at Wilfred, and John said, "Is this getting a bit too much for you?"

The conversation stopped when Alice flicked her head up. Two sticky lines of blood stretched away from her eyeballs in thick tendrils. Her sharp head movements sent a pendulous swing through her loose jaw.

"Jesus," Wilfred whispered as he stared at the lines of claret that ran down each of her cheeks.

She then vomited blood onto the table in front of her. It covered most of the white surface and spilled over the sides. A splash echoed in the room as it hit the floor.

Hot saliva gushed down Wilfred's throat, and a slow heave rolled through his ample gut. When his legs wobbled, he rested on the cold wall next to him to steady himself and turned to look at John.

The scrawny man watched on with childlike fascination; excitement shimmered on his face. "Watch this, Wilfred," he said. "This is the best bit." With his long index finger, he tapped gently on the glass.

A snap of her head, and Alice looked in the direction of the door. She then jumped to her feet; the chair shrieked as it skidded away from her and crashed to the ground. The loud slap of her hands as they slammed down on the tabletop echoed around the room like a *mini thunderclap as she pushed herself to her feet. It took all of Wilfred's concentration to hold onto his bladder.*

John smiled, pressed the intercom, and said, "Come to Dada." Speakers in the room amplified his voice.

Alice twisted her head with sharp movements as she searched for the source of the noise. Her long blonde hair swung out with every turn of her neck. Wilfred gasped when he saw the trails of blood that ran from her ears. When he looked down to see a dark red patch spread through the crotch area of her white trousers, a hot wave rushed through him and his stomach turned over. "Good god."

John laughed in a low murmur. "She doesn't know where we are." He tapped the glass again.

She located the second sound and sprinted straight for them. With her arms windmilling, her mouth wide and dark with blood, she ran face first into the observation window with a deep crunch.

She fell to the floor.

Wilfred looked away and dabbed his watery eyes with the corner of his sleeve. He took several deep breaths to try to pull his heart down from his neck. When he looked back up again, he stared at the explosion of red on the reinforced glass window.

Inside, Alice remained on her back. She rolled and writhed on the hard linoleum floor as if she didn't understand how best to use her limbs.

"Look at it, Wilfred. Beautiful, isn't it?"

Every muscle in Wilfred's body fell slack as he looked at the man. "Her! Not it!"

The bony scientist shrugged.

The disease had made Alice clumsy, and she scrabbled like a spider on ice as she got to her feet again. Heavy breaths rocked her body before she screamed. She ran straight at the window again, hit it head first, and fell back to the floor.

"There's no way this door's giving, love." John laughed as he turned to Wilfred. "It's designed to withstand an atomic blast... literally. No one's getting in, and no one's getting out. At points, there's been information in here that, in the wrong hands, would give The East a huge advantage over us."

Wilfred already knew all of this. Maybe things weren't as safe as John thought they were. He didn't need to tell him that; he'd find out soon enough.

"Also,"—the tall scientist pointed along the corridor that led away from his living quarters—"that corridor is broken up into four bomb-proof sections. Even if she gets through one door, there's no chance she'll get through all of them."

After he'd raised his thick shoulders in a shrug, Wilfred asked, "So what now?"

"We observe. I want to enjoy this because we won't get permission to test on a human subject again."

"And you're confident that you can find a vaccine?"

"Of course, Wilfred. I'm The West's leading germ warfare scientist."

And don't we bloody know it! "You know that we had permission to test this on anyone, right?"

John nodded.

"So why her?"

The reply came back in an instant. "I like a challenge."

It was all about him and his huge fucking ego. "A challenge?" Wilfred cleared his throat and took a step back. "But, John," he said, as his eyes watered more than before, maybe from the fact that he even had to say it. "She's your wife."

***

Rhys pulled the parking brake up for what felt like the thousandth time. The traffic barely fucking moved. "Why do we go through this every morning?"

The lethargic Dave took a few seconds to respond. "Go through what?"

Rhys threw his hand in the direction of the city on the other side of the river. "This bullshit; we sit here like mugs every fucking morning, moving an inch at a time, just to get to work."

"Yeah, it ain't exactly Disney World."

"What's Disney World got to do with it?"

A shrug of his broad shoulders, and Dave smiled. "The queues are worthwhile at Disney World." He pointed across the river. "There ain't no fucking rides over there."

Rhys looked at Summit City and shook his head. It made sense to have a centralised government complex where the entire country's needs were met and administrated, but they'd made every building identical. "One hundred and twenty identical fucking towers."

"What about The Alpha Tower?" Dave said. "At least they got creative with one of the buildings."

The Alpha Tower sat in the dead centre of Summit City. "I'm going to find out what goes on in that building if it kills me."

After a long yawn, Dave nodded across the river. "You'd think they'd build a few more bridges to get over this damn moat. Eight doesn't seem like anywhere near enough. It makes rush hour a fucking nightmare."

"You think they would have made them wider too." Rhys drove a few feet forward and stopped again. "Whose bright idea was it to funnel a seven-lane highway onto a two-way bridge? The city may be a shining example of modern architecture, but you've got to get into it first."

Dave snorted his agreement with Rhys.

A look to either side revealed the deep frowns on the faces of the other drivers to Rhys. He suddenly felt the discomfort of his own scowl. The same angry expression of those around him locked his own face tight. He should be used to the traffic by now. "It's not like it's a surprise that there's queues at this time of day, but the wait still pisses me off."

When one of the cars in the queue beeped their horn, Rhys slammed his palm into the centre of the steering wheel. He held the horn until Dave grabbed his arm and pulled it away.

"Dude," Dave said, "hangover!"

Several more toots called out in the bumper-to-bumper traffic, and Rhys watched Dave flinch at every one of them.

While he rubbed his temples, Dave groaned. "It's not like pressing the horn will get us to work any fucking faster."

"No shit, Sherlock."

"All right, mate, don't take your shitty mood out on me. I thought I was supposed to be the one with the hangover. I'm sorry you didn't see your boy, I truly am. Hell, I want you to see him every time we pass, but don't take it out on me when that doesn't happen. It ain't my fault."

"If you were on fucking time for once, it may have fucking helped."

Silence filled the car.

Maybe it wasn't fair to take it out on Dave. It had much more to do with Larissa dropping Flynn off at inconsistent times each day, but why should Rhys be the one that always gets mugged off?

"Are you sure you weren't having another quickie while I waited in the car like an idiot? You probably had a right good laugh with Julie about the fact I was sitting outside." Rhys jabbed his finger to his temple and said, "Do you even consider that I want to try and see my boy in the mornings?"

The fight left Dave and he offered a soft reply. "Of course I do, mate. I'm sorry. I really don't do it to piss you off."

Rhys looked across the river again at the concrete jungle and ground his jaw. Four square miles of government administration. The heart of the country's infrastructure all in one fabulously erected industrial mecca. The place even won awards for its ambition—it should have received an award for the most monotonous place to work on the planet. He needed to change the subject. "The city fills me with dread every time I look at it. The traffic jams are like a slow march to my death. With each passing minute, I move an inch closer to my coffin-like pod in Building Seventy-Two. What's the fucking point of it all?"

"I get ya, man," Dave said. "Some days I feel like I'm watching my life tick away." The seat creaked as Dave stretched his leg out to pull his phone from his trouser pocket. After a couple of taps on the screen, he held it up to show Rhys.

Rhys glanced at it. "It's a timer."

"A countdown," Dave said.

"To what?"

"Friday at five."

A heavy sigh, and Rhys shook his head. "I fucking hate Mondays."

***

At the end of the bottleneck, Rhys forced his way onto the narrow bridge. He stared straight ahead and kept driving. The game of chicken seemed like the only way to get on. Politeness didn't have a place here. Just before the cars crunched into one another, someone would yield. It was usually the person who looked across first… or the person with the nicest car. It was rare for Rhys to be either.

A horn beeped behind him and Rhys looked in his rear-view mirror. The red-faced man tailing him waved an angry fist. Rhys smiled. "Look at that idiot. Someone thinks they should be allowed on the bridge before me."

Dave turned around and gave the guy a thumbs up.

The guy lost the plot. His face turned a deeper shade of red, and he beat the shit out of his steering wheel. Rhys laughed. "Someone's a bit tetchy this morning. He probably doesn't even know why he's rushing. Honestly, who wants to get to work to start another dull week?"

The road opened up in front of Rhys, but the guy remained on his bumper. The urge to slam his brake on twitched through Rhys' right foot. He sped up instead.

The line of towers in front of them stood in a militant formation throughout the city. Their tinted windows glistened in the sun, and their uniformity made for an imposing skyline. They stood like an indomitable army, resolute and immoveable.

It took Rhys back to when he first started working in the city. "It took a month before I remembered which building was mine. The receptionists must get so fucking tired of giving people directions when they get lost."

"I still pretend I'm lost."

Rhys glanced at Dave then looked back at the road again. "You do?"

Dave's face lit up. "Have you seen some of the receptionists working in the towers?"

Rhys shook his head and rolled his eyes. Then he smiled. "Yeah, I have."

***

Halfway across the bridge, The Alpha Tower came into view. White with totally blacked-out windows, it stood out from all of the other buildings. That and the fact it was at the dead centre of Summit City. The city seemed to have been made to support it, as if it had been built around it. "One day I'll find out what happens in that building."

Dave leaned back in his seat. "You've already said that. You say that every day."

"That's because I will."

"No, you won't." Dave looked out of the side window and said, "I'll tell you what though, it always makes me feel super uneasy going over any of these bridges. Knowing they're all strapped up with explosives, ready to blow should they need to block access to the city. Imagine if it happened right now."

When Rhys looked down at the river below, his stomach lurched. "I'd rather not. Although, I'm pretty sure this bridge is the one that wouldn't go."

"You believe there's one they wouldn't blow up?"

"Yeah, and this is the only one that's a drawbridge."

"So they could still lift it while we're on it? The end result of us two hurtling toward the river in a metal coffin would be the same."

"Yeah, but why worry? What control do we have should they want to do it?" Despite his words, unease churned through Rhys' stomach.

"The question I want to know is why would they need to shut off access to the city in the first place?" Dave said. "I get that we're locked in another cold war, but with the arms embargo, there's no way anyone's getting weapons into the city."

"I know what you mean. It's not like there's a threat from terrorists. What will they come armed with… pea shooters?"

Dave laughed. "Exactly; you couldn't move a weapon anywhere on the planet nowadays without some scanner picking it up somewhere. Any hint of weaponry and it's game over. The big red button gets pressed and it's a full-on nuclear strike."

"Surely we're safer now than we've ever been?" Rhys said.

Dave shot a puff of air through his lips and shook his head. "If you ask me, I think it's all a load of bullshit. If the last cold war taught us anything, it's that it's no more than a pissing contest."

"Too true. It's posturing just to make sure one side leaves the other one alone. We're all fucking terrorists; it just depends which side you look at it from."

Dave removed his glasses and straightened in his seat. "If the two sides can keep their people living in fear, it keeps us compliant. They're probably in on it together to make their lives in government a hell of a lot easier. Keep the people scared; that's the way to keep a society ordered. Moreover, because we aren't allowed to make weapons, we send men into space just to prove our technological prowess. This cold war won't end until there's a fucking flag on Mars, or a gerbil on Jupiter, at the very least."

When Dave sat back, Rhys laughed. A lot of the stuff that came from Dave's mouth made sense, but he often took it too far. "And there it is; the world according to Dave." Although he didn't turn to face his friend, he could sense the two fingers that had been raised in his direction.

A glance to his right, and Rhys looked at the driver of the car next to him. The man sat with the same posture as his and stared straight ahead. Every car moved at the same speed. Every driver sat in virtually the same position.

"You know what though? The thing that scares me so much more than the threat of an all-out war, is that it won't happen. That the next thirty years will pass and I won't know where it's gone. I'll still be fighting for custody of my thirty-six year old son, and I'll still be working this shitty job."

"Why don't you quit?" Dave said.

"For the same reason that you don't see me out with the boys on the weekends; I need the money. This job pays well. Not well enough to get me a good solicitor, but a solicitor nonetheless. This custody battle would take even longer if I earned less money. The thought of being able to see my boy more often, of being able to have him stay over once a week and make him breakfast on a Sunday morning, of being able to go on holidays with him—that's why I do this. That's why I do everything I do. It's all about Flynn."

When Dave's heavy hand landed on his shoulder again, Rhys straightened his back and stared straight ahead. It's all about Flynn.

Chapter Three

For twenty minutes, Wilfred stood in the corridor with John and listened to Alice attack the door. Every time it went quiet, he breathed a relieved sigh and his pulse settled. Then she returned with more venom than before as she growled, screamed, and pounded against the small window.

When the quiet persisted, Wilfred walked to John's side and peered into the room. The glass had turned slick with blood. It threw a red filter over everything.

They watched Alice, lost in her own private hell as she paced the room. When she crashed into a chair, the loud screech made her turn on it. She dropped into a defensive crouch and snarled at the inanimate object.

John laughed. "Look at that. She's scared of a bloody chair."

Violence coiled in Wilfred's muscles, but he swallowed it down and continued to watch Alice.

As if taken over by another surge of rage, Alice snapped her jaws and screamed. An arch of her back, and she roared at the ceiling. Blood sprayed into the air.

"Do you think she's in pain?" Wilfred asked.

With a shrug of his bony shoulders, John said, "Probably."

The man didn't have a shred of empathy. He should be the one on the other side of the door, not Alice. Several hard gulps did nothing to banish the lump in Wilfred's throat. She didn't deserve this.

The intercom buzzed when John pressed the button, and his cold voice came through the speakers in the room. "There, there, my dear. Now listen to me."

She stopped still, tilted her head to one side, and shuffled up to the glass. It seemed that her frenzied mind still recognised her husband's voice. When she was just an inch away from them, she stopped. It was the first time she hadn't crashed into it.

"How does she know where the door is?" Wilfred asked.

"I don't know. Maybe she can see."

"Through bleeding eyes?"

A shrug, and John turned to Alice. "We'll have a cure for this, my love. When we do, you can congratulate yourself for having helped your country. The vaccine will mean we can drop the virus on The East and end this Cold War. You're an integral part to keeping power in The West."

John had never been more compassionate to his wife. One of the few guests at their wedding, more as a witness than guest—a lab partner in an experiment—Wilfred had watched John recite his vows as if they were an apparatus list for the most basic experiment. For the entire service, he wanted to scream for it to stop. He'd have treated her so much better than John ever could. John behaved as if marriage to his beautiful bride was a necessary inconvenience, at best. Alice had tears in her eyes the whole day. When Wilfred asked her why she'd married John, she said she loved his wonderful mind, and she wanted to learn from him. She realised they were the wrong reasons but lifted her ring and said, 'Bit too late now, isn't it?'

When Alice hissed, Wilfred recovered from his daze. She pressed her forehead against the glass and bit at the air.

Playing a part in this heinous act, no matter how unconsciously, had sealed Wilfred's fate. When his time came, he'd be judged for his actions. He took several steps back and arrived at the end of the corridor by the second reinforced door. "So, we need to use this area for quarantine?"

"I wouldn't worry, Wilfred." John knocked on the glass and Alice snapped at his movement. "This door can survive an atomic blast."

With a swipe of his card through the reader, Wilfred watched the light turn from green to red, and the door slid open. John seemed oblivious.

After he'd stepped through and closed the doors behind him, Wilfred listened to the click as they locked. The finality of the sound tied a weight to his heart. Sure, John didn't deserve anything else, but he was about to end this man's life.

As if he'd heard Wilfred's thoughts, John turned to him and his eyes narrowed. "I'm ready to come out now, Wilf."

For the first time since Wilfred had met him, uncertainty hung from John's words. He'd never called him 'Wilf'. After he'd cleared his throat, Wilfred sighed and looked at the floor. "I'm afraid that isn't going to happen."

A glance at the security camera in the hallway with him, the one currently trained on him, and John looked back at Wilfred. "Now come on, Wilf, don't be silly."

"I'm sorry, John, I really am, but they need to study how this virus spreads."

The slight pink hue to John's skin vanished and his grey face sank. "What about my research? How will you find a cure?"

"They have your research. They've been copying it for months now. They always like to have a backup in case something goes wrong."

John marched toward the door and lashed his bony fist against the glass. It did nothing. "How can you do this to me? You're supposed to be my friend!"

Like he knew what the word meant. "We need another subject for this experiment, John." Wilfred's voice shook and his face burned. "When you chose your wife to test this thing on, you showed that you weren't someone to be trusted. If, in the name of science, you're prepared to do this to her, then what would you do to us if the need arose?"

John pressed his long bony hand against the glass. "Wilfred, wait! There are things in my head that no one knows." He jabbed a skinny finger at his temple. "It's in here. I have the cure."

Grief buckled Wilfred's mouth. "You understand that it's not me making these decisions, don't you? I didn't even know about this experiment until you'd sat down with Alice. The only reason I agreed to come down here was because I thought I might be able to stop it. But now I've seen what you've done to her…" Wilfred sighed again and rubbed his temples with a shaky hand.

"But who'll find the cure? I know this virus inside and out. No one else will discover it." A vein throbbed at John's temple and his eyes widened. "You need me!"

"There's no doubt that you have a great scientific mind. The best I've met."

John nodded. Wilfred didn't need to tell him that.

"But in your quest to understand the world, you've lost what it means to be human. Your lack of empathy makes you a liability."

The glass steamed up when John pressed his face to it. "Please let me out! Don't kill me! I can win this war."

Wilfred shook his head. "At what cost, John? You've just killed your wife! She deserved so much better than you."

The panic left John's face as he stared at his colleague. "So that's what this is?"

"What are you talking about?"

"Alice. You're jealous that she chose me."

Wilfred shook his head. "Shut up. You deserve to die. You're a murderer."

"That may be true,"—crow's feet spread out from his eyes as they narrowed and he lowered the tone of his voice—"but you're not, Wilf. You don't kill people."

The statement drew a sharp knife across Wilfred's stomach and emptied his guts on the floor. His head spun and he looked away. John was right.

"Can you live with killing a human being, Wilfred?"

Wilfred pulled away and leaned against the wall next to the door. He couldn't look at John anymore.

"Come on, Wilfred," John said. "Please let me out. Please."

The security camera in Wilfred's section looked down at him. The orders that he'd been given repeated through his mind; 'John needs to be infected. We need to see how it spreads'.

"No!" Wilfred shouted as if in response to his own thoughts. "No. I can't do this. John's right; I'm not a murderer. I can't be a part of this!"

The camera shifted slightly. They were watching; of course they were watching.

"Thank you," John said, relieved.

"I'm not doing this for you." A bitter taste rose into Wilfred's mouth and he spat on the floor. "I'm doing it for me. I don't want this on my conscience."

A high shrug lifted John's scrawny shoulders. "Whatever your reason, it's the right choice."

If Wilfred never had to look at John's face again, it would be too soon; but he couldn't kill him. He removed his keycard from his top pocket and swiped it through the reader. "Your judgment will come, John. However, it's not up to me to make it."

The door didn't open.

John's eyes widened. "What's happening, Wilfred?"

With a shaky hand, Wilfred swiped the card again. The tiny red light on the box stayed red. Repeated swipes returned the same result. "It's not working."

"What do you mean?"

"It's not working—my card, it's not working." Wilfred looked up at the camera and said, "We have a problem! My card isn't working."

The camera stared back. The only sign of life in the cold eye was a shifting darkness behind the lens as it zoomed in.

Every muscle in Wilfred's body sank, and he turned to John. "I'm sorry."

The door behind John clicked and popped open.

John ran at it, but he was too slow. It flew wide and knocked him backwards. Alice burst through and crashed into the opposite wall face first.

John sat up and shuffled away. He got to his feet, but Alice was quicker. She careened into him. He screamed, and they both crashed to the floor again.

A guttural growl.
Jaws snapped.
A broken windpipe.
Blood.
Lots of fucking blood.
Silence.
The raw meat didn't seem to bother her now.

***

On his third lap of the multi-storey car park, Rhys squinted against the inky gloom. As he drove, he squeezed the wheel, and his knuckles ached from his tight grip. "What's wrong with this damn place? The sign said there's a space up here, but I'll be fucked if I can see it. I think they report a space when someone requests their car, but not when they've driven off. Do you remember when we were circling a car park the other week for nearly half an hour?"

The previously lethargic Dave had removed his sunglasses completely and sat alert next to Rhys—or as alert as anyone could after a heavy night out. He then pointed to a dark corner. "There it is."

It took a few seconds for Rhys to see it about thirty metres away and hidden between two large cars. "Wow, you'd think I was the one who was pissed last night. Although... that space looks pretty damn tight."

They had to pass the entranceway to get to the space. When Rhys followed the line of Dave's pointed finger, he saw the light above it was red.

"Someone else is on their way up," Dave said. "You'd best be quick, fella."

The screech of Rhys' tyres echoed as he accelerated towards the only parking space on that level. "There's no way I'm losing that space, Dave. No fucking way."

Several sharp turns of the wheel may have sent the car on a zigzagged path through the tight lanes, but it clearly did little to bother the hungover Dave, who leaned back in his seat and sighed. "I don't know why I'm relieved about you finding a parking space. Monday's suck arse. I think I'd rather drive around this car park all morning."

The heralded car hadn't appeared yet, but Rhys put a little more pressure on the accelerator anyway. "I know what you mean, man; especially since I'm going to have to see Clive and Larissa after another happy weekend with my son." While he ground his jaw, Rhys threw the car into the right-angled bend. All four wheels screeched over the sticky tarmac floor.

"You must want to knock the arsehole out every time you see him. I don't know how I'd deal with someone else raising my child."

On the final straight, Rhys looked down at the speedometer. It read forty-five miles per hour.

"You might want to ease off a little though, fella."

With the space just metres away, Rhys pushed it up to fifty. He then slammed the brakes on and the car skidded. The loose items in his boot clattered into the back of the rear seats.

After a few seconds and several heavy breaths, Rhys looked across at his friend. Dave stared back at him with wide eyes. The smell of burned rubber hung in the air. "Clive cares about Flynn. That's what I need to focus on. Besides, my marriage broke because I fucked up. I have no one but myself to blame."

As Rhys pulled into the space, he checked his rear-view mirror to see the car had finally arrived on their floor. He laughed. "Too late now, loser."

The loud scratching sound of metal against metal pulled Rhys' shoulders tight and he slammed the brake on again. "Fuck it!"

Dave sat upright and stared at the Volkswagen Rhys had just hit.

Rhys reversed and lined his car up better the second time. After he drove it back into the tight space, he switched the engine off and his entire body sank. "Fuck it! That's the last thing I need this morning."

When Dave didn't respond, Rhys got out of the car and looked at the scrape on the Volkswagen's bumper.

As he stood there, Dave appeared at his side and glanced around. "There aren't any witnesses, mate. We could move the car to a different space and pretend it never happened."

"There isn't another space up on this floor, and I'm not sure I can cope with another bollocking from Clive about being late because of these fucking car parks. Besides, if someone whacked my car, I'd really want to know who did it. It's a bit of a shit move to just leave it, don't you think?"

"Everyone does it."

The voice of his mother came alive in Rhys' head—If everyone jumped off a cliff, would you do it?—Without replying to Dave, he leaned into his car and removed a notepad and pen.

When Rhys saw Dave stare at it, he shrugged. "I like a notepad and pen in my car. Old habits die hard. It's a good job

I have this though. It's not like I can leave a note on a tablet and slip that beneath the windscreen, is it?"

Dave smiled but didn't respond.

As he rested on the roof of his car to write the note, Dave peered over his shoulder and breathed in Rhys' ear. "Are you sure this is the best way to go, man?"

Now they were out of the air-conditioned car, the heat hung heavy around them. The reek of stale booze and Dave's body heat added to Rhys' discomfort. Rhys tensed up and moved a step to the left. "I'm giving them my details. It's the right thing to do."

"What is it about you and doing the right thing?"

"I've done the wrong things too many times before. It never works out."

There was a twinkle in Dave's eyes. "I do the wrong thing at least three times a week with Julie and it always works out for me."

With a shake of his head, Rhys continued to write. "Why don't you just ask the bloody girl out? You take her for granted, and you know you'll be gutted when she finally gets fed up with your bullshit and moves on to someone else."

Dave patted Rhys' back so hard it stung. "And on that note..." Dave said. "Thanks for the lift, mate; I'll see you at five."

When he held his clenched fist at Rhys for a bump, Rhys stared at him for a moment.

"Don't leave me hanging, bruv."

It may have lacked enthusiasm, but Rhys fist bumped him all the same. "See you at five, mate."

After he watched Dave leave the car park, Rhys saw the car that had followed them up. It seemed to be doing pointless laps like he and Dave had been. How long before it gave up? Rhys then slipped the note beneath the windscreen wiper of the car he'd bashed into and walked away. What a shitty start to the day.

Chapter Four

Wilfred clamped his hands so firmly over his ears, it hurt his head, but it didn't shut out the sloppy crunch of one person eating another in the neighbouring corridor.

After a few minutes, the sound stopped. When he looked up, he saw Alice with her forehead pressed against the window. She licked the glass repeatedly. With John already down, she had her eye on Wilfred next.

"No!" Wilfred shouted as he stared at her bloody glare. His shrill cry bounced off the walls of the empty chamber. After he'd rubbed his damp cheeks and sniffed the snot from his nose, he shuffled away from the door. When he hit the corner of the space, he stopped. Pressed into the cold, hard wall, he breathed in the reek of disinfectant and turned to see Alice still pressed against the window. A deep heave lifted bitter acid up his throat when he saw the lumps of flesh stuck around her mouth.

Then she turned away and left a thick print of blood behind.

Seconds later, John crashed into the window and stared down at him. Wilfred covered his face. "No," he said again, but the image had already been imprinted on his mind. John's piercing blue eyes were buried beneath a film of blood that ran claret tears down his pale cheeks. A snarl hung from his limp features.

Pain swelled in Wilfred's chest and stomach. He couldn't have done anything to help Alice. John, on the other hand…

The white corridor blurred through Wilfred's tears, although he still saw enough to make out the deep gash in John's chicken neck. He still saw the crater in the side of John's head where his ear used to be.

Wilfred clenched his jaw so tightly his teeth hurt. Spittle shot from his mouth when he pointed up at the security camera and said, "How dare you do this to me? How dare you drag me into this mess?"

The camera turned toward him.

"That's right!" Wilfred shouted. "Stare at me from behind a lens, you fucking cowards!"

His raised voice seemed to stir up Alice and John. Both bloody faces pressed into the glass and banged against the doors.

"You'll be judged when your time's up. You'll pay for this with your souls!" Wilfred got to his feet and walked over to the camera until he was directly beneath it. Too high for him to grab, he stared up and shouted, "And before that, you'll be judged in the courts. Permission was given for one death. One!" He threw an angry arm in the direction of the door. "John wasn't an accident. John was murder! Murder that I realised should have been prevented. But you wouldn't let me. I realised it was wrong, and you overrode me. You're the ones to blame, not me!"

The camera moved away as if it had stopped listening. It left Wilfred with the sound of his own ragged breaths and the bangs on the window.

As his fury died, he looked back up at the camera. It had focused on John and Alice.

Suddenly, Wilfred understood. Warm urine soaked his trousers and he looked back at the doors that held Alice and John back. He muttered, "Oh shit." The red light on the door's' control panel turned green.

The doors opened.

***

The hot sun didn't help Rhys' Monday morning fatigue. The warmth of the day seeped into his reluctant muscles and encouraged him to stop, so when he saw his work tower, he almost ground to a halt. The guy who had designed Building Seventy-Two—and every other tower in Summit City—had been inspired by an old building in London called The Gherkin. The retro design looked out of place in the modern city. Not stylish or kitsch, just out of place.

All the towers stood tall and glistened in the sun. They looked like the offspring of stalagmites and mirror balls. In the right part of the city, at the right time of day, one could witness the sun's light as it cannoned through the streets like a pinball. A few years back, when things were still good with him and Larissa, Rhys took Flynn to one of those parts of the city and watched his little jaw drop. It felt like a lifetime ago now.

As Rhys got closer to his building, he caught sight of The Alpha Tower. It had been constructed in the heart of the city and stood in the middle of a huge open square. The square contained about twenty benches and one water fountain. Rhys had taken Flynn to have lunch in the square on the same day he'd shown him the glistening towers. They sat on the small concrete wall that surrounded the water fountain.

The best kept secret in all of Summit City, The Alpha Tower hid its truth behind thick security doors, dark windows, and white finished steel. The city existed because of it. The buildings around it served as a way to divert people's attention from it. Whatever mysteries hid inside, they were clearly dangerous enough to set Summit City up so it could be quarantined at a moment's notice. A moat and bridges wired to explode—a city that performed simple administrative duties had no need to be so paranoid.

With his attention on the tower, Rhys didn't see the large man until he collided with him. The contact knocked the man's tablet from his hand and it fell to the floor with a crack.

"I'm sorry," Rhys said as he watched the man pick his device back up. "Is it okay?"

The man laughed. "Of course it's okay,"—he knocked on the screen and shrugged—"you can drop these things onto concrete from ten metres and they'll be fine. Watch where you're going though, eh?"

"Sorry."

As Rhys got closer to his building, he looked up at its impressive height. When he craned his neck, his head spun. Made up of twenty-five identical floors and one ground floor, Building Seventy-Two—and all of the other buildings in Summit City—made Rhys feel like an ant on a giant chessboard.

If only he had Flynn's wonder for the city. Although it felt like an age ago when he'd brought his boy here, Rhys remembered every detail of that day; he became a Summit City tour guide. Flynn gasped when he found out that the city handled every bit of government administration for the entire

United Kingdom. It had been constructed in record time; although since its construction, Dubai had built their own complex in a quicker time and on a grander scale. They'd even constructed the island they'd built it on. That put Flynn on a momentary downer.

When Rhys' phone vibrated in his pocket, he pulled it out and looked at the display. He didn't recognise the number—it had to be the owner of the Volkswagen. A deep breath did little to settle the tension now in his stomach, but he lifted the phone to his ear anyway. "Hello?"

It was a man's voice. "Is this the moron that bumped my car?"

After he'd let the silence hang for a moment, Rhys finally replied, "I wouldn't say moron—"

"I would."

Although he clenched his jaw, Rhys kept his tone level. "A moron would have scratched your car, walked away, and not left a note. I was tempted to be a moron, but that wouldn't have been the right thing to do, would it?"

"You could have tried not bumping into it in the first place."

A deep sigh, and Rhys said, "Thanks for the advice. Next time I make a mistake, I'll pull my time machine from my pocket and just rewind by a few minutes. How does that sound?"

"You're lucky I don't put a fucking brick through your windscreen, you moron. I've had to come away from my desk because my alarm alerted me to the fact my car had taken damage. My boss is pissed."

Rhys pulled the phone away from his ear and stared at it for a few seconds. His thumb shook as he hovered it over the red 'end call' button. After another deep breath, he pressed it. The guy can wait; fuck him. What would Dave have said had he witnessed that conversation? Whatever it was, the words 'I told you' and 'so' would have been in there somewhere. Sometimes, the way Dave lived his life seemed like the way to go. He never worried about doing the right thing. He did what was right for Dave and seemed pretty fucking happy because of it.

As Rhys stepped up to his building, he saw the queue in front of him and muttered, "Fuck it." The line for the retina and fingerprint scanners stretched all the way out the doors.

About thirty people deep, the queue could have been worse. The security guards watched the people as they passed through, but no one had been pulled to one side. When they got on one of those kicks, the queue would be three times longer.

***

Despite how much he blew on his coffee, it still burned Rhys' lips when he took the first sip. Larissa had often joked about him having an asbestos mouth. It didn't feel very heat resistant at that moment.

Rhys swiped his security card through the reader on his desk and stared at his computer screen.

"Please make sure you're at eye level," the female voice prompted him.

The screen turned into a mirror with a red line that ran across the centre of it. A quick adjustment of his seat allowed Rhys to follow the machine's orders.

"Now, please lean back in your seat so it fully supports your back. Remember how important it is to maintain good posture and take regular breaks."

The regular breaks thing he could live with. The good posture thing, not so much. An entire day of sitting with a straight back was neither natural nor comfortable. But what could he do? Slouch and the posture alarm went off. The medical team had given him far too many warnings as it was. After he'd leaned back into his seat, Rhys waited.

"Thank you. Scanning retinas… Scanning retinas… Scanning retinas…"

Before the process could complete, Clive and Larissa's voices entered the office. It pulled Rhys' attention away from the screen.

"Please face the screen. Please face the screen." The alarm-like voice rang out for everyone in the office to hear.

Panic turned Rhys clumsy as he snatched at his security card and ripped it from the slot. IT would send him a warning for that one. Every time an employee removed his or her security card, it was to be only after the computer was logged off. Better to receive the condescending letter than let his computer tell his ex-wife and her lover that they were being watched.

Not that it bothered him to see Larissa and Clive together. Well, okay, it did bother him; it tore at his heart every day, but she had a right to move on. Besides, it wasn't like he could ever have a relationship with her again. Too much bad blood ran between them, and it wasn't worth living a life of misery so he could wake up in the same house as Flynn each day. It wouldn't be healthy for Flynn. With a tense stomach, he took another sip of his coffee as he watched the pair kiss. He looked away before they'd finished.

In his peripheral vision, he watched Clive head in the direction of his corner office, and Larissa came over to her pod. Rhys had met Larissa at work. They'd had adjoining pods for a year or so before they started to date one another. Since they'd split up, they'd remained at the same desks. What else could they do? The only way to change desks in this place was to be fired, die, or get promoted. Some people stayed in the same pod until they retired. A few died without ever moving desks. Old Ryan Bell died *at* his desk; the same one he'd had since the day he'd started.

With Larissa fucking the boss, there's no way she was going to get a promotion; it just wouldn't be fair. And they wouldn't promote Rhys. If he got paid more money, he could get a better solicitor. But they couldn't fire him either—that wouldn't look good on Clive. Nope, Rhys was fucked. He was destined to die a slow death in his cubicle as he watched his ex-wife and his son's new dad play the happy fucking family and grow old together.

When Larissa disappeared behind the temporary walls that made up her workstation, Rhys threw a timid, "How's Flynn?" in her direction.

As he awaited a reply, he listened to her move things around on her desk. She crashed and banged on the other side of the partition.

"I said, how's Flynn?"

Never one for a scene, Larissa kept her voice low. "Jesus, Rhys, I've not even turned my computer on yet."

The caffeine had added rocket fuel to Rhys' veins and his pulse raged. Despite this, he managed to keep his reply level.

"All I'm asking you is how my boy's doing. I've not seen him for over a week. It's not unreasonable to ask." In the past, they would have argued. Not now though. It didn't serve any purpose and would only give her ammunition to take to their eventual court battle for custody of their boy. When Rhys drew a breath to speak again, Larissa cut him off.

"He's fine. He's doing great, in fact. He had a wonderful weekend."

The weekends Flynn spent away from Rhys were always wonderful.

"Clive and I took him swimming," Larissa continued. "He's doing widths now without arm bands. Clive's such a good teacher, and Flynn loves swimming with him."

Sure, Clive was now with Flynn much more than Rhys could ever be, but that didn't make him an arsehole. He was a middle management moron who spent a bit too much time with his head in an inspirational manual and not enough reading the reactions of his staff, but he had a good heart and he did genuinely care about Flynn. "I'm pleased Flynn's happy. Thank you for telling me about the weekend; I'm glad you all enjoyed it."

When Larissa didn't reply again, Rhys picked up the photo of Flynn from his desk. Time had curled the corners of the image, but did nothing to diminish the depth of his boy's brown eyes. People had told him they had the same eyes, not that Rhys saw it. Instead, he saw the warm smile of his boy. Everything else may have been a disaster in his life, but when he looked at Flynn's smile, Rhys could overcome whatever came his way.

He placed his card back in the card reader on his desk and

returned his attention to the mirrored screen.

The computer started its routine again, and the female voice said, "Please make sure you're at eye level."

Chapter Five

"We had to do it, Frank."

Unable to move his sore eyes from the monitor, Frank still hadn't blinked when he said to Artem, "We didn't have to do anything." He flinched as he watched John and Alice tear into the portly Wilfred. Alice, who seemed to have earned alpha status already, went for the neck, while John attacked one of Wilfred's ample thighs.

After he'd cleared his throat with a wet cough, Frank added, "Wilfred didn't deserve that."

The only light in the room came from the monitors. Artem's fingers danced over his keyboard. He remained focused on his screen when he said, "All of the other doors are fine. The locks are solid. They're safely quarantined up there."

Frank looked across to see Artem with his hand raised for a high five. A shake of his head, and Frank returned his attention to his own monitor. "There's nothing to celebrate."

Once the other two had finished with Wilfred, they left him limp on the floor. As Frank continued to watch, his mouth dried. The anticipation of what was to come sent a hot wave of nausea through him. Sweat lifted on the back of his neck.

First, Wilfred's left arm twitched. Then his left leg jumped from the floor. His head thrashed from side to side. He snapped at the air, but his body didn't seem to have worked out how to move yet. As Wilfred lay on the floor, he released a throaty, phlegmy growl. The sound turned Frank's skin to gooseflesh.

Frank shook his head and said, "I know they're in the penthouse, and we're about as far away as we can possibly be in this building, but it still feels too close."

When Artem laughed, Frank tensed and his shoulders lifted into his neck.

"You're paranoid, Frank. We're in control here. There's no way this is—"

A loud pop rang out and Frank looked across to see Artem crash onto his keyboard. Blood covered the monitor in front of him. Before he could turn around, Frank felt the hot end of a gun barrel press into the soft patch just below his right ear. He tilted his head around as far as the gunman would allow. "What the—"

"Don't look at me," the man behind him said. He had a thick Chinese accent. "Keep your eyes on the fucking screen if you want to live."

A surge of adrenaline pulled Frank's stomach tight. He lifted his shaky hands in the air. "O… okay. Sorry."

The man behind pushed so hard it felt like he was trying to drive the barrel of his gun through Frank's skull.

"Ow!"

"Shut up, pussy."

When Frank blinked, a tear fell onto his desk. "What do you want?"

The man pulled the gun away, and Frank relaxed. A sharp pain then exploded across the back of his head; the loud crack made his ears ring. Before he had time to shake the dizziness, the barrel of the gun returned to the soft patch below his ear.

"You don't ask the fucking questions! Got that?"

Frank nodded.

The butt of the gun hit the back of Frank's head again, and the loud crack made his world spin. "Yes," Frank said as he rubbed the sting on the back of his head. "I've got it."

"I just want you to know that your wife, Juliette, and your two boys are okay."

Frank's stomach lurched. "What have you done to them?"

Another blow and Frank blacked out for a second.

"Are you fucking deaf or something? You don't ask the fucking questions! They're fine. That's all you need to know. If you do everything I ask of you, then that's how it will stay. Fuck me over, and we'll kill them. And I don't just mean a bullet through the head."

The man leant so close to Frank that he could smell cigarette smoke and his breath tickled his ear. "We'll make rats eat through your boys' stomachs. Your wife will be forced to watch it while my men take turns on her."

Tears soaked Frank's cheeks, and a shudder ran through him. "Anything," he said as his lips trembled. "I'll do anything you want."

The man pointed his gun at the screen. It showed a family of four in one of the building's lifts. "Take control of that lift. Stop it there."

Clumsy with fear, Frank hit several wrong keys.

The gunman pushed the barrel of his gun hard into Frank's head again. "Don't fuck about. Hurry the fuck up!"

Frank shook like he had hypothermia and typed as quickly as he could. A quick check of the monitor showed him the family had gotten closer to their destination floor. Just before they arrived, he hit enter. The lift stopped.

Frank released a stuttered sigh and swallowed against his dry throat. He wiped the sweat from his brow. "There."

The pressure beneath his ear eased off slightly. "Good. Now redirect it to the penthouse."

"But they have children with them!"

The next blow made a wet pulse throb in Frank's ears. The taste of his own blood filled his mouth and he gulped a huge swill of metallic saliva. A wet heave threw half of it back up his throat. He swallowed it back down, and the bitter taste made him shudder.

"Well?" the man demanded.

Frank slurred his words. "You've got to stop hitting me; once more and I'll be done for."

The barrel left the spot beneath his ear and Frank flinched as he waited for another blow.

It never came.

The man behind him calmed down. "So, I have you on side?"

Frank nodded.

"I swear your family are fucked if you mess this up. Eight of my boys are sitting in your front room right now with them."

The man put his phone in front of Frank. It took a few seconds before Frank made sense of the image. Men surrounded his family with more weapons than a small nation. Another gulp of his own blood, and Frank said, "Okay. I'll do whatever you need me to do."

"Redirect them to the penthouse."

The little girl, the youngest of the family, couldn't have been any older than three. A doll hung limp from her hands and her jaw hung loose as she stared around the lift. Her brother played a game on a phone. More tears rolled down Frank's face as he typed on the keyboard and pressed 'enter' again.

The lift came to life. The family inside visibly relaxed and the dad hugged his daughter.

When it passed what was clearly their floor, the dad pressed the button on the panel. At first, he pressed it hard. Then he jabbed it. Before long, he hammered it repeatedly.

Frank's sweaty fingers flew over the keyboard and he managed to hit 'enter' before the dad pressed the emergency call button. When the dad pressed it, it did nothing.

As the family elevated, the man in the room with Frank said, "You know who we are?"

"I'm guessing you're from The East."

"Check you out, brainiac. The accent gave me away, huh?"

Frank shrugged.

"We found out about your little experiment going on today; about your plans to drop it on us."

"I wouldn't know anything about what they'd planned to do with it."

"Bullshit! It doesn't matter though. When we're done, you'll wish you were dead. You'll probably wish your family were dead too."

Frank's entire body tensed. "Leave my family alone. You said you wouldn't do anything to them if I did as you say."

"And I won't, Frankie-boy. I won't." His voice dropped to a low hiss. "You'll wish I had though."

***

The walk from Building Seventy-Two to the square only took five minutes. Despite the short distance, by the time Rhys had sat down on the wall that surrounded the water fountain, sweat had stuck his shirt to his back.

At least he had the comfort of his old trainers rather than his work loafers. He'd left his tie in his top drawer and shoes beneath his desk. They were items for the subservient. A necessity while in Building Seventy-Two, but no one could tell him what to do on his lunch break. At work, he would often remove his shoes and not put them back on until the end of the day. It was a 'fuck you' to the bosses... an act of rebellion that gave him a small sense of freedom. People may have given him strange looks when he walked around the building in his socks, but fuck what other people thought.

Ian, the office pedant, had gone as far as to suggest *no shoes* went against health and safety. Ian could go fuck himself. The look Rhys gave him at the time conveyed that thought. The jobsworth never brought it up again.

The sound of running water helped coax the tension from Rhys' body. Just one morning in the office wound him up tighter than a guitar string.

The air always seemed fresher in the square. Rhys filled his lungs and the warmth of the strong sun sank into his skin.

Rhys looked at the people on the benches. From where he sat, he had a clear view of the entire square. It always filled up when the sun came out. As the only open space in Summit City, it provided an escape from the labyrinthine maze of alleyways and roads. A large patch of grass would have topped it off perfectly, but Summit City was a pure concrete jungle.

As always, Rhys faced The Alpha Tower. The matte black windows had a heavy tint to them that stopped anyone seeing in. From how dark they looked, it probably stopped anyone seeing out too. One day, Rhys would find out what went on in there. Something utterly unremarkable, no doubt—either that or the person who told him would be duty bound to kill him afterwards. A smile twitched at the sides of Rhys' mouth. Like there would be anything that exciting in Summit City.

Rhys lifted his small rucksack onto the wall beside him and unzipped it. He removed the photo of Flynn from the back pocket; it was the one he'd had on his desk earlier. He stared at his boy's dark brown eyes. He never went anywhere without the photo. "I love you, mate; don't forget that."

Rhys removed a lump of tree bark next. It had been painted in the way only a child knew how. The layers of paint, laid one on top of the other, had turned it a muddy purple. The varnish added a contradictory smooth finish to the rough item. The bark served as the perfect paperweight, so he laid the photo down next to him and placed the bark on top of it.

When he pulled his clear lunchbox from his bag, he popped the lid and peered inside. Sometimes, a morning spent in transit could make his lunch look like it had been through the spin drier. Today, his ham, cheese, and tomato sandwiches had remained in tact.

The second he took his first bite—the bread slightly soggy from the tomato that had been in it all morning—Rhys' phone buzzed in his pocket. He put his sandwich down. If it was the guy about his bloody car again… no way would he let that angry idiot ruin his lunch break.

It was a text message though; the notification on the screen sent a pang through his chest. The angry idiot would have been miles better. Before he clicked 'open', he stared at the heart next to her name. He should really change that in his list of contacts.

He pressed his thumb against the print scanner on the screen and his pulse raced before he'd even read the message.

I'm sorry, I forgot to tell you earlier, but you can't see Flynn this weekend. Something's come up.

Something's come up! Something always fucking comes up. The mouthful of sandwich suddenly tasted bitter. He typed his reply. *What do you mean, 'Something's come up'?*

Before he'd put the phone back in his pocket, it buzzed again. *He wants to go to the zoo.*

Perfect, I'll take him to the zoo then.

No, sorry, Clive has already booked the tickets, and he's sooooooo excited to go with him. :)

Like a fucking smiley face made everything okay. And of course he was excited; he was six years old and someone had promised to take him to the zoo. Unless she meant Clive; if she did, Rhys couldn't give a shit about Clive's excitement to go to the zoo.

The brief interaction had turned Rhys' stomach to acid. With his phone in his hand, he looked at the water next to him. If he threw it in, it would only make his life harder in the long run, but it would stop that bitch from intruding with bad news any fucking time she wanted. A look down at the picture of his boy and he took deep breaths.

After a minute or two, Rhys replied. *Please tell Flynn I love him. I think about him every day and I'm so proud of him.* There's no way Larissa would reply, and very little chance she would even tell Flynn, but he couldn't do anything else. He had to keep his head. He had to do the right thing. Until the custody case had been settled, Larissa played the drum and he danced like a monkey for peanuts. In the past, the state would have helped him with his legal costs, and a decision would have been made by now. Then a newly elected government decided legal aid should be withdrawn from child custody cases. Poor families clearly didn't deserve justice. Now he had to rely on a shit lawyer who seemed utterly disinterested in his plight. Something as simple as giving a father access to his son, and he had to go skint forever to achieve it. No matter what happened though, he wouldn't give up the fight for his boy.

***

Bile boiled in Rhys' stomach and the few mouthfuls of sandwich he'd already eaten rose up his throat. Not only had that bitch ruined his weekend, but she'd ruined his lunch too. After he put his sandwiches back in his bag, Rhys picked his phone up again. His hands shook as he opened his emails and started a new message.

To: Shannonwalk@walkthelinesolicitors.com
From: Rhysloveslols@smokingmail.com

Subject: Flynn - What else?

Dear Shannon,

Please find below the latest interaction between myself and Flynn's mother. She's cancelled on me AGAIN! That's FOUR times in the past three months. I'm only allowed to see him once a fortnight as it is! You said I have to play by her rules until we sort this, but I'm finding it damn hard. I should be seeing him more already, but nothing's happening.

Please push this case through quicker. I'm desperate to see my boy more often!!!!!

Beneath the message, he cut and pasted the conversation between Larissa and himself before he hit send.

Before he'd returned the phone to his pocket, it buzzed with a reply.

To: Rhysloveslols@smokingmail.com
From: Shannonwalk@walkthelinesolicitors.com

Subject: RE: Flynn - What else?

SHANNON IS OUT OF THE OFFICE UNTIL THURSDAY THE 24th. IF YOU HAVE ANYTHING THAT NEEDS URGENT ATTENTION…

Bile lifted into Rhys' throat and he couldn't read beyond that point. It seemed like his solicitor spent more time on holiday than she did at work. Although, with the money she charged, she could probably afford holidays every two fucking weeks. An image of her as she drank cocktails by the pool made Rhys' blood boil. Before he could launch his phone, he shoved it back into his pocket and looked at the photo of his boy again.

Chapter Six

Frank watched the screen until the lift reached the penthouse.

"Now open the doors." Although the voice of his captor had moved farther away, Frank had no doubt that the gun remained trained on him.

Frank input the command and hit 'enter'. The doors to the lift opened.

The family stumbled out and looked around. The sterile environment clearly confused them. Then they saw the scientists… A door separated the family and the diseased. The little girl screamed. The boy looked up from his phone. As one, the family stepped back into the lift and the dad pressed the buttons. The lift stayed where it was.

"They look hungry," the voice said. "Now let them out."

"What?" Frank asked.

"Do I need to hit you again?"

When Frank hesitated, the man said, "Think of your family. My men haven't had sex in a long time. Abstinence keeps them sharp, although I am prepared to let them indulge if I need to."

Frank typed. He had to work by touch because his vision had blurred through his tears. 'Enter'.

The final set of doors between the infected and the family slid open. The scientists charged forward.

The dad stepped out and held his arm up in front of him… one last noble act as the protector of a wife and children.

Alice bit a huge chunk from it as she drove him backwards into the lift.

The family screamed.

Wilfred and John crashed into the lift seconds later.

The screams soon stopped.

With the diseased and the yet to reanimate family all bundled in the lift, the man said, "Close the doors."

Chunky sick rushed up into Frank's throat, and he vomited on the floor next to him. After he'd wiped his mouth with the back of his sleeve, he quickly typed and pressed 'enter'. The doors closed.

"Now send them to the foyer. Once you've done that, we're getting out of here. Both of us can make it out." The whistle of a launched object culminated in keys landing on the desk next to Frank. "We'll both have time to escape. You'll have time to get to your family."

Frank pulled his car keys close. He looked up at the ceiling and drew a deep breath. Thank fuck! He'd virtually left his seat by the time he'd finished his final command. 'Enter'.

Frank jumped from his seat, and the chair scooted out behind him. The man with the gun had already left.

After he threw the door wide, Frank headed for the car park. Good job the man had given him his own keys so he could escape. Fuck knows how he would have found someone else's car.

The thought of the lift on its way to the foyer spurred him on.

He had to get out before they did.

His lungs burned as he ran.

The taste of sick and blood lined his mouth.

He burst outside.

The car park for The Alpha Tower had been built on the other side of the road.

As he weaved in and out of the traffic to the sound of horns and fury, he got his car keys ready.

When he pressed the button to unlock the car, his hazard lights blinked once.

In one fluid movement, he opened the driver's side door, slid into the driver's seat, and put the keys in the ignition.

Tyres screeched and Frank watched the black Mercedes with tinted windows flash past. It ploughed through the exit barrier. The wooden arm splintered on impact.

Frank turned the key.

Then he saw the wire hooked into his ignition.

"Fuck!"

The flash blinded him.

The roar deafened him.

The heat burned him.

***

Rhys couldn't be sure how long he'd sat there and stared at the photo of his boy; time suddenly didn't matter.

The explosion near The Alpha Tower shook the ground and sent ripples through the water in the fountain. Screams filled the air as panic ignited in the busy square. Rhys stared in the direction of the sound.

About fifty metres away, at the edge of the square, a thick mushroom cloud of smoke rose up into the sky. It came from the direction of The Alpha Tower's car park.

Rhys looked around and saw most people had gotten to their feet. When he saw Jake, the young lad from the post room, the boy's eyes widened and he mouthed, 'What the fuck?'

Chapter Seven

Rhys stood slack-jawed and watched the smoke as it rose into the sky. Streaks of flames pushed it higher and bridged the gap between the noxious emissions and the recently exploded car that had created them.

A crowd formed closer to the explosion and blocked Rhys' view of the car. Some onlookers still yelled and screamed, but for most part, the panic had abated.

Jake from the post room jogged over. "What's happening, man?"

Rhys watched the crowd grow larger near the car and shrugged. "I'm not sure. It's calmed down pretty quickly though, so maybe there's a perfectly rational reason for it happening."

"A reason for a car exploding?"

It did sound a bit far fetched.

Most of the people in the square had stood up. Some even climbed up onto the benches. But like Rhys and Jake, very few went any farther forwards.

"How the fuck does a car just blow up?"

Before Rhys could respond, the screeching of car tyres grabbed his attention. A sleek black car with tinted windows accelerated away from the square. Rhys couldn't see inside. When he saw Jake watch the car too, he said, "Who do you think's in it?"

With a slack jaw, the slightly gormless teen watched the car speed off. "Dunno, but whoever it is, they clearly want to get away from here."

Another scream called out across the square. Its shrill pitch lifted a line of hairs on the back of Rhys' neck.

"It's coming from The Alpha Tower," Jake said.

When someone else by The Alpha Tower screamed, Rhys stood up on the wall that surrounded the fountain.

A second later, Jake joined him. "What the fuck?"

Despite the distance, Rhys saw it too—or rather, her. "She can't be any older than six," he said as he looked at the doll that hung from the little girl's grip. "Where are the guards on the door?"

Jake looked at him. "Huh?"

"The Alpha Tower security's so tight, there's no way she should be able to just walk out like that."

"I don't think that's our biggest worry, bruv. Look at her."

The slant of the girl's shoulders made it look like they'd been put on wrong. Each movement twitched and jerked as if a spate of erratic electrical impulses controlled her. Blood surrounded her mouth. Her thin lips drew back; she hissed and snapped at the air around her. Two thick trails of blood ran from her eyes down her cheeks. The crowd backed away. "Why isn't someone helping?" Rhys said. "She's just a kid. She needs help."

With a tug on Rhys' sleeve, Jake jumped down from the wall. "Come on then, let's go and see what's going on."

When Jake pulled on his arm again, Rhys followed him off the wall and toward The Alpha Tower at a jog.

The closer they got to the tower, the denser the crowd. People loved a drama, although no one wanted to go and help her. When Rhys saw an unoccupied bench he called, "Jake" and jumped onto it. Jake followed his lead. The city usually fined people who stood on the benches. They probably didn't give a fuck about that right now.

For a moment, everything else vanished as Rhys stared at the girl. She swayed with heavy breaths and watched the crowd. The sheer amount of people didn't seem to faze her at all. She held her ground as if she could take them all on.

When she exploded to life, Rhys damn near fell from his perch...

As the girl charged forward, a woman in the crowd screamed. The girl roared in response; deep and guttural, it seemed an impossible sound for such a small frame.

Only a third of the size of the screaming woman, the girl hit her so hard she knocked her over. Even from a distance, Rhys heard the deep bark as the wind left the woman. The child tackled like she was on a rugby pitch.

The pair hit the concrete ground with a loud *thwack*. They disappeared from Rhys' sight because of the dense crowd. He traced their scuffle by the crowd's reaction. A bigger and bigger space opened up as the people formed a ring around the pair. More people screamed as the panic of what was initially only a few spread to those around them.

"What the fuck's happening?" Jake said.

A gap opened in the crowd, and Rhys saw the girl had bitten into the woman's neck and remained clamped onto it. Several people, fully-grown men and women, surrounded the girl. They tugged on her legs but they couldn't pry her free. "I think we should go, Jake."

A loud foghorn silenced Jake's reply. It boomed through the city and echoed off the hard surfaces. It rang so loud it blurred Rhys' vision and hurt his ears.

The building on Rhys' left went first. Brushed steel shutters snapped across every window in quick succession. It turned the pillar of shiny brilliance into what looked like an industrial phallus. Surrounded by a protective shell, it seemed that not only had the windows been covered, but every entrance and exit. Nothing could get in or out.

All of the other buildings followed suit. The collective snapping and sliding of barriers called out through the city like some kind of mechanical army as it suited up for battle. Within seconds, the noise had stopped. It seemed like every building had gone into lockdown—every building *except* The Alpha Tower.

Rhys turned full circle as he took in his surroundings. "They've shut down Building Seventy-Two, Jake."

"My car keys are in there."

"Mine too," Rhys said.

"What's happening, Rhys? Have you ever seen this before?" Rhys shook his head. "Never."

Another loud *snap* and a cylindrical steel pillar shot up from the middle of the road closest to Jake and Rhys. About half a metre tall and thirty centimetres in diameter, it blocked the way for any vehicles that would try to escape. Like the buildings before it, the sound repeated throughout the city. It sounded like popping corn as all of the pillars came up at slightly different times.

"Whatever's happening," Rhys said, "I guarantee you it's got something to do with—"

Screams by The Alpha Tower cut Rhys off. When he looked over, anxiety twisted through his bowels. The woman who had been attacked by the girl had gotten her feet. Like the girl, her eyes bled. She bit at the air like a dog trying to catch flies. Blood oozed from the deep wound in the side of her neck. The crowd screamed again when she snarled. She ran at the person closest to her. Driven by the same rage as the small child, she crashed into her victim, and they both fell to the concrete.

The little girl stood up too. Within seconds, she'd taken out a man like she had the woman before him. No one tried to help a second time.

The muscles in Rhys' legs tightened. If he was to get out, it needed to be now.

When he stepped down from the bench, Jake looked at him. "Where are you going, man?"

Rhys shook his head as he backed away. "I dunno. Away from here though."

Chapter Eight

The sound of panic chased Rhys as he jogged away from the tower. A deep growl rode beneath the shrill cries and screams. Something guttural and tormented, it sounded like the little girl, but multiplied. Rhys quickened his pace.

Most people hadn't twigged yet and stood dumbstruck as they stared in the direction of The Alpha Tower. As he weaved in and out of them, one girl called to Rhys, "What's happening down there?"

Rhys ignored her as similar questions came at him from the other onlookers.

"Why are you running?"

"Why are the shutters down?"

He couldn't stop to answer them. Even if he could, they wouldn't believe him. If they hadn't seen it with their own eyes, surely they wouldn't go for the idea that a little girl had just bitten the throat out of an older woman. He couldn't convince them to run.

The deep growls and yowls increased and provided a low bass line to accompany the shrill chaos. Rhys gritted his teeth and picked his pace up another step.

Before long, Rhys ran at a flat-out sprint. It didn't matter that people stared at him. Let them. The questions came at him from all angles, and all centred on the same theme—*What the fuck's happening?*

The farther Rhys got from The Alpha Tower, the more sedate the crowd. A lot of people stared at him still, but the questions died down.

A man, with his phone raised to record the chaos, stepped out in front of Rhys. With only a second to react, Rhys clipped his shoulder. The impact ran a sharp pain through him, but Rhys didn't slow down. He heard a *crack* as the man's phone hit the ground, followed by the man releasing a barrage of abuse at him.

***

When Rhys reached the edge of the square, he stopped. His lungs burned and his heavy breaths rocked his tired frame. The crowd outside The Alpha Tower had gone from panicked onlookers, to a writhing mass of insanity. Whatever happened back there, it spread fast and would catch up with him if he didn't keep moving.

Rhys looked but couldn't see Jake. The poor kid probably didn't make it out. They would have been better had they remained on the wall by the fountain.

Rhys looked back at the water fountain and his bowels sank to his knees. "Fuck!" He knew that on the wall, exactly where he'd left them, sat the bark and the photo of Flynn. If Jake hadn't have been so damn keen to get involved, he would have never left them there. "Fuck!"

An older woman stared at Rhys and said, "Are you okay? What's going on back there?"

Did he look okay? Instead of responding to her, Rhys rubbed his face with both hands and shouted into them, "Fuck!"

When Rhys felt someone grip his shoulder, he pulled his hands away. The older lady raised her eyebrows at him. "Please, tell me what's happening. Why were you running?"

With a quick shake of his head, Rhys pulled a deep breath into his tight lungs. He stared into the lady's wide eyes and said, "I've seen hell, and it's coming this way."

The woman's gasp chased after Rhys as he ran full tilt back toward the insanity in the square.

Chapter Nine

A quick side step and Rhys dodged the guy whose phone he'd knocked to the floor only minutes previously. He, and those around him, stared in the direction of The Alpha Tower. They still hadn't got the message to get the fuck out.

Every instinct Rhys had told him to turn around and run the other way—every instinct other than the one in his heart. He couldn't leave that picture behind.

Random sprays of blood shot into the air; screams, growls, hisses, and roars filled the square. Whatever was happening, it was brutal, and it had spread fast.

A group of people ran straight at Rhys. The crowd finally seemed to have woken up. With his sights fixed on the water fountain, he dodged and sidestepped through them. Half of them looked over their shoulders as the chaos chased them. Some of them screamed. Some cried.

Another loud explosion like the one that had started it all ran through the ground. It threw Rhys slightly off balance and he crashed into another person as they fled. He remained on course for the fountain and looked for the source of the explosion. He saw nothing.

A girl in her teens ran straight at Rhys. She looked over her shoulder and Rhys had no choice but to raise his forearm. When she turned around, his elbow smashed into her nose. A wet crack, a shriek, and she crashed to the ground. He'd hit her so hard, the pain made his entire arm weak.

With the fountain less than twenty metres away, the circle of carnage that radiated from The Alpha Tower grew.

Yet another explosion tested his tired legs, and Rhys wobbled again. He narrowly avoided another collision. The explosions drew louder screams from those around him. Snippets of people's fear entered Rhys' world.

"What is it?"

"…like bombs."

Rhys fought for breath as another explosion went off.

"Terrorists?"

"The East?"

Another explosion.

Then another.

It could be terrorists. The East dropping bombs on them. Everyone saw it coming. Rhys scanned the sky, but it was as clear and blue as a child's painting. Its purity stood in stark contrast to the furore below. There were no missiles up there.

Another explosion.

A woman from The Alpha Tower—blood-red eyes, features twisted with hate—collided into an old man directly in front of Rhys. They both went down, and the bloodied woman dove into the old man's neck with her mouth open wide. Without a break in stride, Rhys jumped over the downed pair. The man on the floor screamed. Within seconds, he became just another cry of many.

Two more explosions came so close together they almost sounded like one.

"That was two," someone in the crowd called out.

Ten metres until he was at the fountain.

Another explosion.

"That's seven in total," someone else said.

"Seven?" The conversation seemed to catch as if everyone in the square were having it.

"It's the bridges. We need to get out of here before we get trapped in the city."

The few who remained static burst into action and added to the swell of escapees.

Rhys clattered into person after person as he fought against the mass exodus.

When he arrived at the water fountain, his body battered from his run against the mob, Rhys lifted the bark and photo of Flynn. For the briefest second, he stared into his son's dark eyes. For the briefest second, everything around him stopped. He slipped both items into his pocket.

Then he looked up and breathed a relieved sigh. "Jake?"

Except it wasn't Jake. Not anymore.

Chapter Ten

Rhys recoiled from the personification of hate and let out a high-pitched yell as he closed his eyes and raised his arms up in front of him.

The expected impact never came.

When he opened his eyes, he saw a woman shoulder barge Jake. It sent him sideways over the low wall that surrounded the water fountain. A popping crack sounded out as Jake's top half went towards the water, but his feet remained in the same place. Jake seemed oblivious to his clearly broken shins. Instead, his twisted features remained fixed on Rhys. His desire to attack seemingly overrode what must have been pain beyond measure. Either he didn't feel the pain, or his lust for the kill burned brighter than anything else. Something inside told him it was the latter and a chill gripped Rhys.

The blonde woman passed Rhys at a flat-out sprint, so he called after her, "Hey, wait up."

She didn't.

For a second, he froze and stared at Jake in the fountain. The boy's legs pointed at impossible angles to his body, and he thrashed and writhed as if he were drowning. A loud roar grabbed Rhys' attention. He saw another one of the crazed people nearby. "Sorry, Jake," he said, spun around, and sprinted off after the woman who'd just saved him. In the insanity that surrounded them, she seemed to be the only person with purpose.

The combination of too much noise and too little air in his lungs made it a struggle to get his words heard, but Rhys tried anyway as he called after the woman again, "Wait up."

She still didn't react.

The crowd continued to flee from the square. At least he didn't have to run against them anymore. Although, with so many bodies, he lost sight of the athletic woman who'd saved him.

The roars of the people from the tower spread. The woman then came back into view as she tore a zigzagged path through the pandemonium, and Rhys tried to keep up.

Rhys gave everything he had, but the woman continued to pull away from him. The crowd thickened and she disappeared from view again.

This far back, no one seemed to know which direction to run. Two people in front of Rhys fell to violent attacks.

A strong grip stung Rhys as it locked onto his shoulder. He shook it off, stumbled, and turned to see the bloody eyes of one of the crazed people. They tripped and fell before they could grab him again.

The sound of his own ragged breaths echoed through his head, and Rhys dug deep as he pushed on. The heat of the day suffocated him, and sweat cascaded into his eyes. It didn't help to run in slacks and a shirt; they raised his body temperature by what felt like a thousand degrees. Thank god he had his trainers on. The woman came back into view through the crowd. She had about a ten–metre lead on him.

An impact stung Rhys' left side and an older lady spun away from him like a top. Her arms and hair flailed out from the collision. She fell and someone jumped on top of her. Before Rhys had passed her, she screamed as the person that had pinned her down bit into her face.

More people got between Rhys and the athletic woman. All of them seemed occupied by their own personal panic. At least a third of them fell to attacks before his eyes as the amount of enraged people multiplied by the second. With raised arms, Rhys shoved anyone who got in his way aside and kept his focus.

When a gap opened up in the crowd again, Rhys saw the woman disappear down a tight alleyway between two buildings.

He hurdled a bench, shoved a man with blood-streaked cheeks away from him, and followed after her.

Chapter Eleven

Rhys burst from the other side of the alleyway and found himself on a road with a line of thick steel pillars that protruded from the ground. They ran all the way down the middle, spaced about five metres apart. Four pillars separated him and the woman up ahead. The gap continued to increase as she outran him. Rhys called after her again. "Wait!"

But she didn't stop.

Sweat stung his eyes, and his head spun from the exertion of trying to keep up with her. "Wait up, please."

For the first time since she'd saved him, the woman turned around and looked at Rhys. She was younger than him, although he couldn't tell how much younger. She looked to be maybe twenty-four.

With a raised hand, Rhys repeated, "Wait, please."

Although she didn't stop, she slowed down enough for him to catch up with her.

Once he was next to her, Rhys wiped his brow with his sleeve and spoke in between gasps. "Thank you… for… saving me."

Her cool blue eyes pinched at the sides as she stared at him.

She breathed evenly. It made a mockery of Rhys' fitness levels.

A scream shot out of the alley they'd just exited. The woman looked back, alert like a rabbit that had sensed a fox. She tugged on his sleeve and pulled Rhys along with her. "We can't wait around here. Can you walk at least?"

After he'd gulped a dry mouthful of hot air, his throat sticky from the run, Rhys nodded.

As they walked, Rhys continued to chase his breath and neither of them spoke. The tall buildings on either side of the narrow road had been built so close together, they stood like huge walls and cast heavy shadows. The steel armour that surrounded each building nullified the illuminating effect of the shiny windows. Rhys had never seen the city this dark before. Another phlegmy roar from the square turned Rhys' skin to gooseflesh.

The pair walked either side of the line of pillars down the middle of the road. Rhys tapped each one as he passed it. They'd clearly been erected to quash even the idea of driving on the roads.

"Did you see how many people ran for the car park as if to get their cars?" the woman said.

"What?!" Rhys tapped another pole. "Didn't they see these in the road?"

The woman shrugged. "Panic turns people stupid."

After he'd slapped two more pillars, Rhys glanced at the woman next to him. She scowled as she took in their environment. When his breath finally returned to him, he said, "It was good of you to save me. You didn't have to. Thank you."

For a moment, she didn't reply. Then she looked at him.

"Why were you running at the zombies?"

The word nearly choked him. "Zombies?"

"Well, that's what they are… or as good as anyway. Didn't you see them?"

Who was this woman? A fine physical specimen, no doubt, but where was her head at? "I thought zombies only existed—"

"In movies?"

"Yeah."

"I remember a line once from an old film—'The greatest trick the devil ever pulled was convincing the world it didn't exist'. By filling you with popcorn and adrenaline rushes, the government kept the 'myth' of zombies alive. They kept them fictional so we wouldn't believe in them. All the while, they were creating them under our noses. They were nearly ready to drop them in The East."

"Okay," Rhys said, "so if they're zombies, why aren't they slow, shuffling, brain-craving deadites?"

"Deadites?"

Rhys shrugged it off.

"It's more like a virus, a disease. They're not reanimated corpses like in the movies; they're infected humans. They may be stronger and faster than your average human, but they die in the same way. There are two effective ways of killing them— serious head trauma or drowning. For some reason, they can't swim. They can't climb either. The virus makes them fast and aggressive, but they lose a lot of control over their limbs."

"How do you know all—?"

Another scream came from behind, and the woman's shoulders pulled into her neck. She quickened her pace. "It's a virus that turns people insane. It spreads through saliva. If you get bitten, you're fucked."

"How do you know all this?"

"I worked in The Alpha Tower."

Rhys stopped. "You worked in there? I've always wondered what went on in there." He resumed his pace and caught up with her again.

"Well, now you know. It's a biological warfare lab." As they walked, she glanced behind, in front, and up at the tall buildings, which flanked their path. If something appeared, she made sure she'd notice it. "I only found this out about an hour ago when soldiers from The East infiltrated the building and set the disease loose. None of them looked oriental. It was only when I heard them speak that I realised where they came from. By then, it was too late. They even managed to sneak guns in."

"Guns? But what about the arms embargo? I thought we knew how to detect weapons."

"So did I; I honestly don't have a clue how they managed it."

"That must have been who I saw driving away," Rhys said, more to himself than the woman. When he saw her looking at him, he explained. "After the explosion, I saw a car with tinted windows speeding away. They looked seriously suspicious. So why a virus?"

The woman shrugged. "Dunno. My only guess is it's a good way around the anti-weapon policy. The East can detect the equipment and processes involved in making weapons and flag them as suspicious, but there are no restrictions on labs, so how could they tell if a virus was being made? That would be my guess anyway."

"And we clearly aren't as clever as them to invent weapons that can go undetected." Rhys shook his head. "What the fuck? We've created fucking *zombies* to try and win a ridiculous war."

"None of that matters now," the woman said. "We've already lost. It's all about survival from this point on. Anyway, you didn't answer my question."

Rhys looked at her

"Why were you running at The Alpha Tower?"

Rhys removed the bark and photo from his top pocket and showed them to her.

Despite her obvious need for urgency, the woman stopped and levelled a dead stare at him. "You nearly killed yourself for a photo and a lump of wood?"

"A photo and a paperweight."

"Why?"

"It's a photo of my boy, Flynn. I don't see him much. His mum only lets me see him once a fortnight for a few hours on a Saturday morning." Sadness gripped his heart. "If I'm lucky, that is. She sometimes cancels. She often cancels. The bitch cancelled this weekend, in fact."

When he held up the bark, he couldn't help but smile at it. "He painted this for me. I take both items with me everywhere. I couldn't leave either of them behind."

The woman didn't respond.

"You think that's stupid?"

"No, I don't have kids, so I can't pretend to understand what it's like to feel that kind of love for someone. I'm just not sure I'd risk my life for a photo."

"I didn't really think of it as risking my life. I was confused.

You don't ever expect a violent disease to spread while you're on your lunch break."

"I do."

Rhys looked across at her.

"Surely you have a plan?"

"Um…" Now he felt stupid.

"Everyone has a plan for when the zombies hit."

Rhys didn't. Fortunately, she didn't push him on the matter.

"So why do you let your wife keep you away from your son?"

"What else can I do? I have to fight it through the courts. I have to do this the right way, and to do that, I have to keep paying my crappy solicitor until they decide they have a case pulled together. Arguing with my ex will only upset Flynn. It's the right way to do things."

"There's no right way now."

"Huh?"

More screams called out from behind them. The woman pulled her long blonde hair back, slipped a hairband from her wrist, and tied it in a ponytail. "Didn't you just see what happened back there? This is going to get a whole lot worse before it gets better. You've seen the movies, right?"

Fear gripped Rhys' stomach. "It's really going to be that bad?"

"Didn't you just see how quickly it spread? This is ground zero. Things are going to get a whole lot fucking worse."

"In that case, I've got to get to Flynn. I have to get him out of school. If we're quick, we can outrun this and get there."

"We?"

"You're coming with me, right?"

The woman winced. "Sorry, but I've got to get my shit together. I'm sure your kid's a lovely boy, but I have my own issues to deal with."

Another scream, louder than before, called out behind them.

"They're getting closer," she said. "Come on, let's go." And with that, she broke into a jog.

Chapter Twelve

Rhys reached out and grabbed the woman's arm. "Please, I need to slow down again…"

Despite her deep frown, she accepted his request and they slowed to a fast walk. "Fine. And it's Vicky, by the way."

It took several deep breaths before Rhys finally said, "Rhys." He tugged on his shirt, but the second he let it go, it stuck to his body again. "I'm going to do everything in my power to save my boy."

The sound of the diseased and their victims screamed behind them. Far enough away to not be a problem, Rhys kept his attention on Vicky.

Vicky looked ahead and continued their conversation. "I know; you've already said."

Both the heat and exercise had turned Rhys' throat arid. A hot gulp did nothing to relieve it. "It's the only thing I can think about doing. It's the obvious thing to do. Flynn's only six years old. I can't possibly leave him in this world on his own."

"No, you can't; he wouldn't last thirty seconds."

Yet she still didn't want to help. "How come you know so

much about this virus? You said you just learned about it an hour ago."

The question made her flinch. When Vicky replied, she didn't look at him. "You can learn a lot in an hour when you watch it tear through a building."

"The right thing for you to do would be to come with me, you know? He's a little boy."

Vicky spun around and pointed an angry finger at him. With the tip of it just millimetres from his face, she said, "Fuck off!"

Rhys threw his arms wide and looked around the deserted street as if he had a crowd of people to appeal to. "What? What did I say?"

Despite her fierce demeanour, a softness dampened her blue eyes.

"You're trying to guilt trip me," she said. "I don't appreciate it. What the fuck do you know about what the right thing to do is?"

"What else do you want me to say?" Grief wedged in his throat like a hot lump of sand. His eyes watered. "He's the most precious thing in my world. I need help saving him, and you're the only person around. I'm desperate."

The heavy frown that sat above her azure glare faltered. "Well, say that then. Don't try to guilt trip me; that ain't going to work."

"I'm sorry," Rhys said, "you're right." After a pause, he held his hand out to shake. When she took it, her grip firm, yet soft, he said, "Let's start again. Hi, my name's Rhys."

"I don't care what your name is."

"That's not very nice. What's your name?"

86

"Vicky. You know it's Vicky; we've been through this already."

Before Rhys could say more, Vicky walked away from him toward a sports shop on the side of the road. Like all of the other buildings, it had a shutter of protective steel. Rhys looked back in the direction they'd come from and then returned his attention to Vicky. "You know that's locked too, right?"

The fit woman spun around and pressed a finger to her lips.

The sound of chaos behind them had gotten louder. Soon, it would be so loud they'd be able to feel the hot breath that came with it—sooner, if Rhys didn't shut up.

Despite his body's reluctance, Rhys jogged over to her, but before he could say something—quieter than before—he saw her remove a security card. When she swiped it through the reader, the light above it turned green, and the shutter rose. The steel clattered as it lifted.

"You have a clearance card?"

When Vicky stared at the card but didn't reply, Rhys' cheeks flushed hot. "Obviously!"

"It's only level B. I can get into commercial buildings, but without another card, I can't get into any of the blocks with most of the people in them. Not that I would want to anyway. I just want to get the fuck off this shitty island. If I released even one building full of people, it would make getting out of here twice as hard. The amount of diseased would double and we'd be fucked. Besides, the towers are controlled centrally. Release one—"

"And you release them all," Rhys said. "So you got the clearance card…?"

"Because I worked in The Alpha Tower; I've already told you that."

Another glance up and down the road, and Rhys still couldn't see any of the creatures. Then a particularly high-pitched cry ran a shiver down his spine. "Whatever you're doing here, Vicky, it needs to be damn quick. Those fuckers will be on top of us before long."

After she'd levelled another dead stare at him, Vicky walked into the shop.

Rhys followed behind.

The lure of the trainer section pulled Rhys over to the far wall. The sheer amount of them made the entire shop smell of rubber.

Then Rhys found it—the same trainer he'd coveted for months, now. Solicitor bills had ruled out frivolous purchases, but money didn't matter anymore... at least not at the moment anyway.

He pulled the trainer from the shelf, tilted the tongue back, and read the label behind it. "It's my size. Surely it's a sign?"

As he laced it up, Vicky turned around and stared at him. "What the fuck are you doing?"

"I've needed a new pair of trainers for months now. I need to make the most of this opportunity to get them."

A shake of her head, and Vicky turned away to look at the wall of bats and racquets on another side of the shop.

The run had left Rhys' socks damp with sweat, but he slid his foot into the shoe anyway and wiggled his toes. Nothing came close to feel of new trainers.

After he'd tied the shoelaces, he walked up and down and

checked how it looked in the little strip of mirror along the floor. When he looked up, he met Vicky's cold stare. The penny finally dropped. "I'm only going to have the right one, aren't I?"

A smile cracked her stern face, and she shook her head.

Rhys pointed at the door next to the counter. "That must lead to the store room. Don't suppose I could—"

"Hang on, weren't you just telling me that we had no time? You think I'm going to risk my life so you can look cool? No fucking way, pal."

The petulant teenager inside of Rhys threatened to rise to the surface, but he managed to push it down. Vicky clearly didn't have a high opinion of him, as it was; the last thing he needed to do was give her justification for that.

"Anyway," Vicky said, "you need to pick a weapon, and we need to get out of here."

"A weapon? What's wrong with running?"

"Nothing,"—Vicky raised an eyebrow and looked him up and down—"if you could do it!"

Rhys shrugged and turned to the wall of rackets and bats. He looked at the shiny aluminium baseball bats and grinned.

When Rhys pulled the fattest bat from the wall, he squeezed the soft grip. He turned the bat to the side and read the writing that ran down its edge. "Slugger series X." With both hands, he wrung the handle as if he'd just stepped up to the plate. "I like it." Now that he had a weapon, he had to man the fuck up. Vicky needed a man by her side, not a scared thirty-something, good-for-nothing office worker.

After she'd stared at his bat for a few seconds, Vicky gave him a nod of approval and selected the one next to it.

"So, what were you into before this, Vicky?"

Vicky cocked an eyebrow at him. "Are you seriously asking me what my hobbies are?"

"Come on, if we're going to get through this together, we may as well get to know one another."

Without response, Vicky walked over to the vending machine and swiped her card through the reader. After several quick button presses, two bottles of water, wrapped in condensation, fell into the tray at the bottom with two loud thuds. She removed one and tossed it at Rhys.

With the bat between his legs, Rhys removed the cap. The cold water burned as he guzzled it down.

It took half of the bottle to quench his thirst. After a wet burp into his hand, he said, "So not only does that card give you high-level clearance, it gives you free food and drink too? You must have had a lot of responsibility in The Alpha Tower."

Vicky drank the water with much more restraint. Their escape had seemed to have very little effect on her. She still didn't respond.

"Okay, so if you're not going to play the game, I suppose I'm going to have to guess." A look up and down the length of her body made Rhys smile. "I'm guessing you worked out; you look pretty fit." She looked damn fit.

Vicky put a hand on her hip and straightened her back. She tilted her head to the side and looked ready to punch him. "And what's that supposed to mean?"

With his hands raised, Rhys said, "Whoa, steady on. What's with the hostility? Let's try and get along, yeah? We can be nice to one another, can't we? Can't I compliment you without you getting the wrong idea?" Not that she'd got the wrong idea at all.

"This ain't about being nice. This is about survival."

It may have been a distant sound outside, but Rhys heard it nonetheless. "Hear that?" he said. "Sirens! The police are going to handle this."

"You don't get it, do you? No one's going to handle this. The army would struggle—let alone a bunch of unfit, donut-munching pigs. This is beyond being handled. I guarantee you that siren's them getting the fuck away from here."

"How do you know so much? What haven't you told me?"

Silence.

Before Rhys could speak again, she cut him off. "I found out about it a year or so ago." The aggression left her words and she looked at the floor. "I never did anything; I just ignored it and continued to go to work. It was a darkness that I pretended wasn't there. A tumour that I hoped would go away of its own accord. But as I understood more of what they were doing, the guilt ate me up from the inside."

She took another sip of water and stared into the distance with unfocused eyes. She had the softest skin, and although stoic, her features spoke of her regret. "If I'd have told someone sooner, then this wouldn't have happened. You talked to me earlier about doing the right thing. I've spent a long time ignoring the right thing and getting on with it. I told myself the usual bullshit. I had bills to pay, it was a steady income, good holidays, medical coverage; but that's all the crap employers give us to keep us compliant, isn't it? So when it comes to doing the right thing, I avoided it like the best of them."

Before Rhys could say anything, she added, "I convinced myself that I played no part in it, but just by working there, I was involved. I had the chance to do the right thing every day and I didn't. So please don't tell me to do the right thing again. As you can tell, it doesn't wash with me."

What could he say to that? "So that's why you had a plan for when the disease broke?"

She almost laughed. "What I knew was I didn't want to get locked in one of the buildings when it kicked off. Those buildings are nothing but prisons now."

"But they keep the diseased out."

"Yeah, and the people in. I'd rather take my chances than trust those in power to act in my best interests. After all, they created this. What if they never let the people out?"

Her words took the breath from Rhys' lungs. "Shit, I never thought of that. I have friends trapped in those buildings."

"Me too," Vicky said.

"So what do we do?"

The blank expression said it all.

Rhys swallowed another mouthful of the cool water. "Okay, so we need to get out, yeah?"

Vicky shrugged.

"But the bridges are down."

"The bridges are down?"

"Yeah. When I was running back into the square, there were seven huge explosions. They were so loud they rocked the ground. What else could they be?"

Vicky chewed the inside of her mouth and peered outside the shop. "I must have been distracted in The Alpha Tower when they blew up. So the only one left is the drawbridge?"

"I knew it was a drawbridge," Rhys said.

Vicky stared at him.

"Never mind." Before she could say anything, Rhys added, "I suppose you're right about the buildings being locked down though. There are far fewer diseased on the street; far fewer creatures between us and Flynn."

Vicky ignored the reference to Flynn. If he pushed her enough, she had to help him find his son. Either that or she'd swing for him.

A scream outside stopped the conversation. Panicked voices came on its tail.

After he shared a look with Vicky, Rhys led the dash to the edge of the shop.

Two survivors ran up the street. They'd come from the same direction as Rhys and Vicky. The grimaces on their faces told Rhys everything he needed to know. He recognised it all too well. "They're fucked. They ain't got much running left in them."

Seconds later, three diseased appeared behind them. Their faces were twisted with hate, and their desire to hunt clearly overrode any exhaustion they may have felt from the chase.

When Rhys stepped forward, Vicky grabbed his arm. "Wait. Let's see if there are any more."

"But those people need our help. We can't leave them. We have to do the right…" He stopped and Vicky glared at him.

Vicky gave it a few more seconds before she nodded. "It looks like they're alone. Let's put these bats to good use."

Chapter Thirteen

Rhys wrung the grip of his baseball bat with his sweaty hands and stared down the street. A deep breath did little for his furious pulse, or the nausea that broiled in his stomach. Regardless, he wound back, ready to swing.

"You all set?" Vicky asked.

Rhys kept his eyes on the chaos that approached them and nodded. "Yep."

The couple held hands as they ran up the street. The man dragged the woman forward.

"Please slow down, Dan," the girl said to what must have been her, what? …partner? …friend? What did it matter? They were fucked if Rhys and Vicky didn't intervene.

The calls and growls of the monsters behind got louder.

"Slow down? If I slow down they'll fucking eat us."

"He's right, you know," Vicky said.

The diseased trio gained on them with every step. The virus seemed to give them some kind of super speed and an unnatural endurance. Driven by hunger, they looked like they could run forever. If Rhys was in that situation, could he leave Vicky behind?

What a ridiculous thought… like he could ever outrun Vicky.

When Dan glanced over his shoulder at their pursuers, he let go of the woman's hand. "What the fuck?" Rhys said. "That ain't right."

"I can't believe it," Vicky said.

The woman clearly couldn't believe it either. His abandonment seemed to rob her of her will to continue. She slowed down instantly, and her frame slumped as she watched Dan run away.

Within seconds, two of the three diseased hit her at the same time. One jumped at her and tackled her around the neck; the other one got her legs, and all three fell.

On their way down, the woman's head bounced off one of the steel poles in the middle of the road. The loud *ping* ran straight through Rhys as he watched her neck snap back.

The third diseased stayed on Dan's tail.

Rhys looked from Dan to the diseased that chased him. He looked back at Dan's writhing love interest. She'd somehow stayed conscious, despite the blow to her head. The two monsters on top of her screamed louder than before, the kill had sent them into a guttural frenzy. The one around her neck opened its mouth wide and bit into the back of her head. The woman lifted her face and screamed.

For a second, she and Rhys made eye contact. A cold dread sank in Rhys' stomach as he stared at the fear in her wide eyes. No one would ever see humanity in her face again.

The diseased forced her nose into the ground as it chowed down. Its head shook from the pressure of its bite. A wet *pop,* and her skull gave way.

Nausea rolled through Rhys' guts. The sound even made the diseased on her leg look up. It stared for a second—its jowls painted with blood and flesh—then it dived back in again.

"Rhys!"

Vicky's call jolted Rhys from his daze, and he watched Dan run straight past them. What a fucking coward. With his bat still wound back, the muscles in Rhys' arms twitched as he waited for the diseased that chased Dan to catch up. In the old world, survival meant he had to work a shit job to pay mounting bills; now, it meant he had to be able to kill.

Despite reluctance turning his arms weak, Rhys swung at the diseased. The metal bat connected with its temple. A shock ran up the handle and a *ping* similar to the sound of the girl's head against the pillar rang out.

The diseased's legs turned bandy, and it stumbled for several steps before it crashed, face first, to the ground. It didn't even try to stop its fall with its hands; instead, it slid along the asphalt road on its cheek.

Something crashed into Rhys' shoulder as it passed him. He raised his bat, but he lowered it when he saw Vicky. She rushed at the downed diseased and swung her bat at its head. The wet squelch made Rhys think of someone crushing a pumpkin.

Several swings turned its skull to pulp on the hot road. The crunch of bones quickly turned into a ping as the bat hit the ground, but Vicky continued to attack the mess of red goo anyway.

When she eventually pulled away, she turned to Rhys. "If you want to stop them, you need to kill the brain."

Rhys looked between the crushed diseased and Vicky several

times before he said, "I think you might have done that."

Vicky flashed a facetious smile, which vanished when she looked down the road behind him. "Look out!"

The two diseased and Dan's lover had gotten to their feet. The same rage of the other two twisted Lover-girl's features. Although, how the fuck she moved with that head wound...

As they bore down on them, Rhys widened his stance, rolled his shoulders, and wound back.

Vicky moved next to him. "You ready for three of 'em?"

"I'm gonna have to be."

The bite to Lover-girl's leg made her run with a limp, so the other two made it to Rhys and Vicky first. One each. Perfect.

Rhys swung for the one at the front. He made contact with its jaw. It diverted the monster past him but didn't knock it down.

When it stopped and turned around, its face hung as limp as its arms. Although gormless in most ways, fire burned in its glare. Before it could run at him again, Rhys took another swing.

He caught its temple and its legs folded beneath it. As it writhed on the floor, Rhys yelled and drove his bat deep into its head. The thing's skull gave way instantly.

The vibration from the asphalt road ran up the bat through Rhys' arms. It sent a sharp pain to his elbows, but he kept going. The thing needed to die now.

The pulped mess on the ground stirred up the metallic reek of blood. It filled Rhys' sinuses and settled on his tongue. Hot saliva rained down the back of his throat, and he swung one last time.

Rhys wiped his brow with his forearm and turned to see

Vicky still engaged in a fight with her diseased. A few more seconds and Lover-girl would be on top of her. "No," he yelled and closed the distance between them with two long strides. He swung for the girl and knocked her down.

After he drove the bat into her head to make sure, Rhys looked over at Vicky.

She panted almost as heavily as him. Then she broke a smile. "Thanks."

The scream of more diseased came from somewhere behind them and cut off Rhys' reply.

Vicky's brilliant blue eyes widened as she stared down the road. "Let's go."

Rhys didn't need to be told twice.

Chapter Fourteen

As they ran, Rhys listened to the footsteps that pounded against the road, the heavy breaths, and the grizzled rattle of fury, or hunger, or whatever the fuck it was behind them. The charge of a thunderous army had picked up their scent, but when he glanced over his shoulder, he couldn't see them yet. Long may that continue; if he never saw them again, he'd be happy. Yeah right! Like that would fucking happen. They were in Summit City; wishes never came true here.

Rhys' lungs burned as he ran. Much more, and he'd collapse before he found safety. They needed to find somewhere to hide. Maybe the creatures didn't have their scent. Maybe Rhys and Vicky just happened to be in their way.

Then he saw it. It took an extra effort to pull level with Vicky, but Rhys did it and grabbed her arm. He then tugged on it to guide her toward the entrance to the multi-storey car park.

At first, she resisted, but when he pulled a little harder, she yielded and followed his lead. Thank god she did; who knows where the next rest stop would have been?

As soon as they ran onto the ramp, Rhys ducked down

behind a small concrete wall. If these things could hunt… well, it didn't bear thinking about. Hopefully the gamble would pay off. As he fought for breath, his heart pounded and his lungs burned. Rhys shook where he crouched and waited.

The sheer amount of concrete that surrounded them dropped the temperature by a few degrees. The smell of damp hung in the air. If the mob that chased them did have their scent, maybe the wet reek would mask it. Whatever happened, Rhys had no running left in him.

With Vicky next to him, both of them held onto their bats and waited as the sound caught up to them.

The rumble of the stampede shook the ground beneath their feet. A twitchiness ran through Rhys' muscles. Vicky's eyes widened and she seemed to hold her breath.

Rhys had made a bad choice. The things could probably smell them. The reek of damp wouldn't do anything to mask their scent. Vicky should have talked him out of his plan. Not that she could, they hardly debated it. Rhys had just led them to their deaths. What a fucking moron.

Exhaustion and fear stole every ounce of energy from him, and Rhys looked across at Vicky again. The run didn't seem to have had an impact on her; she looked ready to go again. If they had to bolt at the last minute, she'd be fine. Rhys, on the other hand… Maybe he deserved it for such a stupid fucking plan. He had to sit and wait now. Wait for them to find him and tear huge chunks from him.

The footsteps rounded the corner. Their collective grunts and groans rode on the back of their thunderous beat, and Rhys' bladder twitched. What if he pissed himself? What would that do to Vicky's already low opinion of him?

Sweat stung his eyes and Rhys continued to fight for breath as he watched the entranceway to the car park. His entire body shook, and his heart beat as if it could explode at any moment. The cold and rough wall stung his back as he pushed harder against it. Armed with hope and a baseball bat, Rhys waited.

Chapter Fifteen

Enough time passed for Rhys to catch his breath. The diseased had gone straight past them, and it remained quiet outside. After a quick glance at Vicky, he stood up and peered over the wall. The bright sun stung his eyes and blinded him. After he'd rubbed them, he looked down at Vicky and said, "It looks clear."

Vicky stood up and peered over the wall too.

Rhys flinched when another scream tore through the city. The mob had taken another victim.

"We need to get out of here," Vicky said.

A quick nod from Rhys, and the pair of them moved toward the exit.

A second later, Rhys grabbed Vicky's arm. When she looked at him, he pointed to an alleyway across the street. The shadows shifted and groaned. Hundreds of the diseased were packed into the tight space.

The pair ducked back down behind the wall.

"They're coming our way," Rhys said. "The streets are too dangerous." His hushed tones echoed in the hard open space of the car park.

Vicky threw her arms up. "Where else can we go?"

Rhys looked at the red door opposite them. It led to the higher levels.

Vicky shook her head. "No way. Why would I go farther into the car park? We're trapped in here."

"At least we have a chance to wait it out if we hide away."

Although she stared hard at him, Vicky clearly didn't have an argument. Rhys took her soft hand. "It's the only way."

She looked far from convinced.

***

When Rhys pulled the swing door open, the hinges groaned. The sound raced up the cavernous stairwell. The hinges as good as cackled when Rhys pushed the door a little wider.

After they'd both stepped though, Rhys closed the door to the same dramatic response. His voice echoed when he said, "What's wrong with a bit of fucking oil?"

Vicky scowled at him.

The stone stairwell allowed access to every floor. As damp as the rest of the car park, the eye-watering reek of ammonia hung in the air. With his nose held in a tight pinch, Rhys shook his head. "How many dirty bastards have pissed in this place?"

The dark expression on Vicky's face remained unchanged.

Each step strained Rhys' weak legs as he ascended the stairs. Vicky followed behind.

As they climbed, Rhys looked over his shoulder at Vicky. She continued to glare at him and made light work of the stairs.

Once they'd passed level three, Rhys broke the silence. "The good thing about those dodgy hinges is they're a dead giveaway if we're being followed. I take the silence as an indication that we seem to have gotten away with it."

"Let's not get too cocky."

Rhys shrugged.

"Where are we going, anyway?" Vicky said.

"Higher ground. If we have a better view of the city, we can plan our route out of here."

"You do realise we're going to the top of a multi-storey car park, right? I mean, it's kind of like hiding in an alley with a dead end. What if they follow us up?"

"Haven't we just had this conversation? Where else can we go? You heard that scream as clearly as I did. You saw the monsters in the alleyway. It ain't safe in the city; at least, not if we're just chancing our luck. We need some sort of plan if we're going to survive this, and I didn't want to be formulating it while I waited for that mob down there to get to the end of their alley."

"We had a plan. Run like the fucking wind until we make it to the one bridge that hasn't been blown up."

"That's easy for you to say." The more Rhys spoke, the less he could breathe. "I don't have the running in me."

"So I have to risk my life because you're a slob?"

"We've got to be smarter, Vicky. This disease is spreading quickly. We can't outrun it."

"You can't outrun it. I can outrun anything if my life depends on it."

"Alright, love, there's no need to be so fucking smug about it."

Vicky looked like she wanted to swing for him.

***

At the top of the stairs, Rhys pulled the door open—quickly this time to bypass any groaning theatrics. He held it wide for Vicky.

For a moment, Vicky didn't move. With her hands on her hips, she looked between the open door and Rhys.

"Oh, right," Rhys said. "It used to be polite to let a woman go first. That was before those things lurked behind every fucking door. Sorry. Old habits and all that."

The bright sun hit Rhys the second he stepped out. The metre-high wall around the outer edge of the car park blocked the wind and turned the place into a suntrap. Black asphalt coated the ground.

Rhys walked to the edge and peered over. When he saw ten or so diseased below them, he drew a sharp intake of breath and pulled back.

When Vicky looked at him, he shrugged. "There's some of them down there. I think we should wait it out up here for a while to give them a chance to clear out."

"But what if they don't?"

"Then we'll be in no worse a situation than we're currently in. What do we have to lose?"

After a pause, Vicky's face softened and she finally nodded. "Okay."

The wall on the opposite side of the car park created the only shade on the entire floor. Rhys moved over to it at a crouched run and sat down with his back against it.

Despite her obvious reluctance with every step of Rhys' plan, Vicky followed and sat down next to him.

"The first thing we need to do is to get out of this city," Rhys said. "Then I'm going to get Flynn. Whatever happens, I'm going to get to him. I know you say you won't come with me, but please reconsider."

Vicky turned away from him.

"You find that works for you?"

Vicky continued to look away.

"The whole ice queen thing; that sees you right in your life, does it? Shut everyone and everything out and make sure Vicky's okay?"

"What do you want from me, Rhys? I've already saved your life."

"But my life's nothing without Flynn."

"Have you considered that Flynn might be,"—she paused—"gone when you get there?"

Of course, he'd thought about it. He couldn't think about anything else. Still, her words drove a knife into his heart. "I have to go to his school. All I have are hopes and prayers. I'll ride their vapours if I need to, but I have to get to his school. Nothing's lost until it's lost."

Vicky didn't reply.

"Come on, Vicky, there's a heart in there somewhere. He's six years old. I need to get to him because God knows I can't rely on his mother. Besides,"—Rhys looked at the buildings that surrounded them; all of which were locked down with steel shutters—"she's locked in Building Seventy-Two. I need you, Vicky. You know how to fight these things."

Although she still had her back to him, Rhys saw her grind her jaw.

Rhys retrieved the photo of his boy from his pocket and reached around to hold it in front of her. "This is him."

She knocked his arm away.

"Go on," Rhys said, "look at him. Look into the warm eyes of my innocent boy and tell me you won't help me save his life. If you can do that, I'll stop hassling you."

When she snatched the photo from Rhys, he flinched.

As she stared down at it, she spoke in monotone. "I don't want to help you save him."

The reply nearly winded Rhys, who took the photo back and looked at his little boy. "You must have been really fucking lonely in your life before this happened."

"What do you mean?"

"To be so switched off. To care so little about anyone but yourself."

She shrugged. "It is what it is."

A shake of his head, and Rhys turned his back on her. "Wow."

Chapter Sixteen

As they sat in the shade, the heat of the day inescapable, Rhys listened. He had nothing more to say to Vicky. It had been a while since they'd heard the call of the diseased, but Rhys didn't want to look over the wall. If the crowd below had grown, they'd be fucked. But if he didn't look, they could end up waiting all day. The longer he waited the less chance Flynn had of survival.

Just as he moved to stand up, Vicky spoke. "You don't want me with you anyway."

"Huh?"

"You don't want me with you. I can't be trusted. I act in my own self-interest. I'm not like you. I don't do the right thing."

Rhys waited for her to continue.

"I knew about this virus well before it was released and I did nothing. I stayed in my shitty job because that was what worked best for me. I didn't give a fuck about what was best for other people." She couldn't even look at him. Her brilliant blue eyes glazed with tears.

Despite the urge to lean across and touch her, Rhys kept his hands to himself. "That's not true; you saved me when you didn't have to. There was no reason for you to barge that diseased into the water fountain, but you did."

"It was in my way."

"If you're so selfish, then why do you keep waiting for me when I can't keep up? You could have left, and you'd probably be on the other side of the river by now."

She looked away and the light caught her high cheekbones.

After a moment's silence, Rhys looked at the floor. "Do you know why I'm not with Flynn's mum anymore?"

"How would I know that?"

"I cheated on her. I had a wife and beautiful boy at home, and I cheated on them. My relationship with Larissa was loveless, and I should have ended it. That would have been the right thing to do. Instead, I got myself to a point where I was so miserable, I was happy to fuck another woman. Instead of taking responsibility for my life, I convinced myself that it was okay to fuck someone else while maintaining the shitty relationship I was trapped in. I haven't always done the right thing either. In fact, it was doing the wrong thing that taught me to change."

"And what happened to the other woman?"

Rhys kicked a stone on the floor in front of him and laughed.

"What's so funny?"

"She's always referred to as 'the other woman'. It's like she's a stereotype and not a person. It didn't work out. Emotions were running too high, and I decided to walk away from it. I was a mess, and she didn't need to deal with that."

He finally looked up and made eye contact with Vicky. He had to look back at the floor so he could speak again. "I've learned from my lies. I'm thirty-four and living on a shoestring budget so I can pay a shitty solicitor to help me see my boy more than once a fortnight. My problems are all my own making."

"So what are you saying? I learn from the fact that I could have stopped humanity's demise? Never mind I played a part in turning the entire fucking world into diseased lunatics. I just move on and become a better person?" A mixture of fury and grief moistened her eyes. "I'll stand up in front of what few survivors there are and apologise for killing everyone they love. But it's okay, everything's great—I'm a better person now." A sneer sat on her face like she had a bad taste in her mouth, and she shook her head.

"What could you have done to stop it? I'm guessing if you'd have threatened to talk, you'd have disappeared very fucking quickly. Just another dead body to be pulled from the river."

Although she stared hard at him, Vicky's face cracked.

Rhys' throat dried and he reached across to touch the back of her warm and soft hand. She flinched, but she didn't pull away.

After a few seconds, she turned her hand over and held his. When she looked up at him, she smiled through the pain. "Thank you."

"For what?"

"For not judging me... for being kind."

"You've done your best in your life and that's all any of us can do."

Vicky nodded.

"You're a good person, Vicky. You need to stop telling yourself otherwise."

She paused for a moment before she looked up. The

starkness of her stare afforded Rhys a rare glimpse at the person beneath the front. "I'll come with you to find Flynn," she said.

A wave of grief rushed forward and made Rhys' skin tingle. He kept a hold of her hand. "Thank you," he said. "Thank you so much."

Chapter Seventeen

Rhys let go of Vicky's hand. They had to move, but they could only do that if the diseased had gone. The top of the rough wall dug into Rhys' grip when he pulled himself to his feet. The second he peered over, his legs buckled and he nearly fell.

Once he'd regained his composure, he tapped Vicky on the shoulder and motioned for her to stand up too. When she got to her feet next to him, he pointed down at the coach below. Caught between two steel pillars, it had nowhere to go. "Look," he said, "a school trip. The pillars have trapped the coach."

The lights may have been off in the coach, but Rhys saw the small bodies that moved inside. When he saw the school's crest emblazoned on the vehicle, he said, "Thank god."

"Thank god?"

Rhys shook his head. "Sorry, I didn't mean that. It's a primary school, but it's not Flynn's."

As Rhys watched the kids move around inside of the coach, he could feel Vicky's attention on him.

"What shall we do?" she said.

"What can we do? We can't rescue a collection of children.

Don't get me wrong, I feel devastated for them, but we can't help them. Flynn's my number one—" The breath caught in Rhys' throat when he saw the diseased man appear.

From the way Vicky tensed up beside him, she'd obviously seen him too. Vicky then whispered, "Dan."

Damn, she was right. Although, not Dan as they'd seen him about half an hour before. Not the man who had abandoned his lover as he ran straight past them. That Dan had checked out, and good fucking riddance. That Dan was a cunt and deserved everything he got.

Other than Dan, there were no diseased that they could see. As he walked closer to the coach, Rhys spoke to Vicky in hushed tones. "I don't think he's twigged that there's anyone in the coach."

It didn't look like Dan had twigged about much as he stumbled along and his head flicked from side to side. He continued to walk toward the coach until he bumped into it. Someone moved inside. Of course they did. It can't be easy to convince a coach full of petrified kids to hold the fuck still. But Dan didn't notice the occupants.

With his sweaty hand clamped across his mouth, Rhys watched Dan slide along the side of the coach. The moistness of his bloody cheek made a *screeeeeee* noise as it ran down the black vehicle's side panel. Dan continued on, and his jaw snapped as if he could taste the air around him. "He knows there's food nearby," Rhys said.

A light flashed in the coach and Rhys' stomach sank. "Fuck!" The mobile phone screen stopped Dan in his tracks.

Rhys' heart ran away with him and his throat dried as he

watched Dan turn slowly and tilt his head up to look at the window. Blood ran over his chin as his mouth hung open. His cheeks ran red.

"How the fuck can he see through those bleeding eyes? How do any of them see through them?" Rhys said.

Instead of a reply, Vicky continued to watch on, her breaths short and sharp.

Hysteria stirred inside the coach as Dan continued to look up. "There must be teachers on there with them," Rhys said.

"Yeah, but how do you keep a coach full of kids calm?" Vicky replied. "It's hard work trying to get one kid to do something against their will, let alone an entire fucking coach full of them."

Another one of the kids moved in the coach.

Dan locked onto it.

Another one moved.

While he stared up at the coach, Dan swayed on the spot.

Another child moved.

"Why don't they keep the fuck still?" Rhys said.

Dan banged on the window.

A child screamed.

Dan banged again, this time with more force.

The movement in the coach stopped.

Dan didn't. Instead, he turned away from the coach and drew a deep intake of air that made his chest swell. Then, with what looked like great effort, he released a primitive scream. Like an enraged chimp, hysterical and fierce, Dan called again and again.

"What the fuck?" Vicky said.

Before Rhys could respond, the rolling thunder of what

sounded like a thousand heavy footsteps replied. Rhys' bowels twinged, and his jaw fell loose. "He's just told the others he's found food."

Chapter Eighteen

The first of the diseased appeared. They ran at full tilt to Dan's call.

Within seconds, the tide rushed forward as a constant stream of them. They screamed and yelled as they descended on the coach.

Vicky's warm hand found Rhys' and he squeezed back.

The first diseased crashed into the side of the coach with a loud *thump*. Several more followed and collided into the side of the large vehicle.

The diseased rocked the coach on its wheels, and more joined them all the time. A lot of them punched it like they thought they could bash their way through the metal.

The high-pitched screams of the children filled the air.

More diseased came.

Rhys gasped when the diseased lifted their side of the coach from the ground. "They're going to tip it."

It landed back on its wheels with a *crash*.

They tried again with the same result.

"They're lifting it higher each time," Vicky said.

When they lifted the coach again, Vicky said, "No."

The huge vehicle yawned like a large beast as it passed its tipping point. For a second, it teetered on its edge.

Then it fell.

It hit the ground to a loud *splash* as broken glass exploded away from it. The diseased jumped onto the side that now faced the sky and pounded against the unbroken windows.

"Don't they have an emergency hammer to break the glass with?" Rhys said. "Surely they should try to do something to get out?"

Hundreds of diseased flooded over the side of the coach like ants onto sugar. They banged against the windows. Anxiety twisted Rhys' stomach. "It won't be long before—"

The windows down the side of the coach popped one after the other. The roar of a feeding frenzy mixed with the screams of what must have been at least forty children. They didn't stand a chance as what seemed like a continuous stream of diseased swarmed out of the city.

The diseased rushed through the broken windows. They pushed and shoved one another aside to get at their prey. A fight broke out between several of them over one little boy who cowered beneath them. Rhys dropped his head and closed his eyes. He didn't need to see any more.

***

When the cries stopped, Rhys looked up to see a writhing mass of activity inside the coach. Tears ran down his cheeks as he looked at the blood that coated the side of the black vehicle. Small diseased children climbed out of the wreckage, dazed and confused as if they'd just woken from the night terrors. With bloody eyes, slack jaws, and jerky movements, clarity had left their tiny minds. "Look at what we're up against," Rhys said. "How the fuck are we supposed to get out of this city?"

When Vicky didn't reply, Rhys looked at her. She cried freely too. With a heavy sigh, Rhys turned away from the carnage.

Then he saw it and every muscle in his body froze.

Chapter Nineteen

A little boy of no more than about four years old stood in the stairwell door. He kept it propped open as he stared at Rhys and Vicky. Other than the twitch of his head from side to side as he seemingly took in Rhys, and then Vicky, and then Rhys again, he stood still. A low rattle ran through his chest with his laboured respiration.

Malice then twisted his features as he drew a deep breath that swelled his rib cage.

"Oh fuck!" Rhys said.

Higher pitched than Dan's, the boy's shrill primitive call sent ice through Rhys' veins.

The child's scream came in three braying waves. It may have only lasted a few seconds, but it felt like a fucking lifetime. Rhys lost his breath when he looked over the car park wall at the carnage below. As one, the pack of what must have been one hundred or more diseased looked up… straight at Rhys. Their collective bloody stare drove frigid dread to Rhys' core.

When he turned to Vicky, he saw it in her eyes. Despite her tough exterior, he knew she couldn't do it.

Rhys headed straight for the boy and wound his baseball bat back as he ran. Just the thought of it weakened his muscles, but one of them had to do it.

The aluminium bat connected with the kid's skull. It only took one swing to extinguish the boy's fury and knock him to the ground.

To make sure, Rhys stamped on the kid's head. His skull gave way like it was made from eggshell, and Rhys heaved at the sound of the wet crunch. Diseased or not, he'd just killed a little boy.

When he looked up, Vicky stared at him. A mixture of pity and disgust played out on her face.

The door to the stairwell creaked when Rhys pulled it open and pointed into it. "Come on, we've got to go if we're to get away." The sound of his voice echoed throughout the cavernous space.

When Rhys stepped over the dead boy and into the stairwell, the door at the bottom crashed against the wall from where it had been kicked open. The scream of the diseased filled the space. "Fuck!" Rhys said.

After he'd jumped backwards into the car park again, Rhys lifted the dead kid's ankles and dragged him out of the way. "We can't go down there, Vicky."

Vicky looked over her shoulder in the direction of the car park next to the one they were in.

As he pressed himself into the now closed door, Rhys shook his head. "No way. No."

"What else are we going to do?" Vicky said. "There's no other way."

The thunder of footsteps accompanied the screams that raced up the stairs. Rhys could feel their approach through the ground. "No way, Vicky. I can't do it."

It clearly didn't matter what Rhys could or couldn't do, Vicky had made her mind up. She bounced on her toes and said, "Just watch me. If I can get across it at my height then so can you."

The ground vibrated to the point where the door rattled in its frame. With his breath caught in his throat, Rhys looked at Vicky and nodded—like he had any other choice.

Vicky took off and ran at the wall on the far side of the car park at a flat-out sprint. Rhys couldn't even move that fast.

The screams grew louder, the diseased so close he could smell their fetid musk of death. No more than two floors separated them and Rhys now.

Vicky didn't break stride when she jumped up onto the metre-high wall that ran around the car park. She kicked off the top of it and flew through the air. No way could she make it. As her arms and legs windmilled, Rhys' stomach flipped and he looked away. He couldn't watch her fall to her death.

Chapter Twenty

When Rhys looked back, he saw Vicky had landed on the top floor of the car park on the other side. She waved him over. "Come on, Rhys, you can do it."

The first diseased that reached the top of the stairs hit the door so hard, Rhys nearly fell over. His shoulder stung when he pushed back against it.

The second one didn't catch him off guard as much, but as the third and fourth threw their weight against the door, Rhys' feet slipped a little. If he stayed there much longer, it wouldn't be a choice if he ran or not, the fuckers would be on top of him as they tore chunks from his face.

The door pushed open a crack. Bloody hands slid through the gap. Diseased fingers brushed against Rhys' right arm.

While he gritted his teeth, Rhys pushed harder against the door, but his trainers slipped over the asphalt.

A variety of hands poked through. From adults' to children's, bloody to muddy, black to white; every one of them had bloodstains. Every one of them wanted to grab Rhys.

While he fought his losing battle, Rhys looked down at the

dead boy. That could be Flynn if he didn't get to him. He had to try to jump.

When Rhys took off, the door flew open and crashed into the wall behind it. Chased by the wet slaps of feet, Rhys put everything he had into his escape.

It sounded like thousands of them spilled out into the car park, but Rhys didn't look behind to check; he didn't need to.

With his baseball bat still in his grip, Rhys ran at a full sprint across the car park. He kept his focus on Vicky and her calls of encouragement.

The footsteps chased him. The footsteps gained on him.

Worry lines creased Vicky's face as she called out, "Come on, you can do it. *Come on.*"

It sounded like rabid dogs chased him. The slathering rattle of bloodlust rode their phlegmy breaths. And the stench! Now they were on the same level, the fetid metallic reek damn near choked him.

Rhys narrowed his focus onto the top of the wall, took three steps, and jumped at it. With his heart in his mouth, he pushed off with his right foot and leaped toward Vicky on the other side.

Just as he left the wall, a hand caught his trailing heel.

Chapter Twenty-One

Rhys snapped his foot away before the diseased's grip could tighten around it. The gap between the two car parks may have been small, but at thirty metres from the ground, it felt a lot larger.

When Rhys hit the other side, his legs gave way beneath him, and he crashed to his knees. The hard ground burned his kneecaps before he fell forward onto his shoulder. A shock ran through his entire body.

He lay on the floor and panted, but he'd made it. He'd damn well made it.

Winded from the landing, Rhys got to his feet with Vicky's help. She wrapped him in a tight hug. The tough embrace aggravated the sharp throb in his shoulder, but he didn't pull away.

When Vicky let go, the pair watched the diseased on the other side. In the few seconds it had taken for him to get his bearings, the mob had swelled to at least seventy strong. They leaned across the gap as if their outstretched arms would be long enough to reach; all the while, more poured through the door behind them.

As Rhys watched the slack-jawed and bloody-eyed diseased at the front, he said, "They're not going to jump across. Let's go before they realise they can cut us off on the ground."

After he'd shown the mindless mob the back of his raised middle finger, Rhys led their escape towards the stairwell on the opposite side of the car park.

Chapter Twenty-Two

The door at the bottom of the stairwell in the neighbouring car park creaked as loudly as the others, if not louder. As Rhys let Vicky through, he held his breath and listened out for the uncoordinated beat of clumsy feet against the ground. After the successful jump, they didn't need to be screwed over by a squeaky door.

While he kept the door propped open with his foot, Rhys pulled a fire extinguisher from the nearby wall and used it to keep the door held open. He looked at Vicky, shrugged, and spoke in a whisper. "If we just got away with opening this noisy fucker, the last thing I want to do is ride our luck by closing it too."

Vicky nodded.

Once outside, Rhys ran to the edge of the car park on tiptoes. He looked up at the diseased that had chased them. They remained at the top of the car park, reaching across the gap between the two structures. He turned to Vicky, who was close behind. "They clearly don't get where we've gone. I hope they won't twig for a while. They may have speed and brutality on their side, but these things are as thick as lobotomised sheep."

When Vicky pointed in the opposite direction, Rhys nodded. With the diseased at the top of the car park, their opportunity to get away had come. Vicky took the lead and Rhys followed close on her heels.

They stopped before they ran out into the road, and Vicky peered around the corner this time. It was just a formality; confirm the place had been abandoned and then get the fuck out.

But Vicky pulled back around and shook her head.

Rhys' heart sank. "What's up?"

Vicky stood aside to give Rhys the chance to look. When he poked his head around the corner, he saw the downed school bus and his entire body slumped. Most of the children had remained close to the vehicle. They'd been conditioned in their former lives to not wander off, and they'd seemed to stay true to that order, in spite of the disease.

Rhys looked back at Vicky and shook his head. "There's no way we'll sneak past them."

With the coach lying in a pool of blood the size of a pond, Rhys watched the twitchy movements of the aimless children.

Nearby screams snapped tension through Rhys' body and he pulled back around the corner. When he looked at Vicky, he saw her eyes were wide and her breathing rapid. "We're surrounded," he said before he added, "Imagine what this city would have been like if the buildings hadn't gone into lockdown."

"That was the point I was making earlier," Vicky said. "We wouldn't have lasted two minutes."

As Rhys searched their surroundings, he frowned. Then he saw it… the underground train station. When he looked back up at Vicky, she shook her head.

"No way."

"But all we have to do is cross the street, and we can get the fuck out of here. Surely we're better off taking our chances down there than we are up here?"

"Have you forgotten there are fucking tunnels down there, Rhys? Imagine getting caught in a tunnel with those things."

"I don't think the diseased are down there," Rhys said.

"And you think we should chance it on a hunch? What if it's full of them?"

Rhys closed the gap between them and grabbed Vicky's soft hands. "We need to keep our voices down." He rubbed his thumbs over the backs of her fingers before he looked into her eyes. "I think it'll be safer down there. Besides, I don't see that we have much choice. Staying up here is suicide."

"It's a fucking tunnel, Rhys. What if we get cut off from both ends?"

Another scream made Rhys jump, and he let go of Vicky's hands. His voice shook and his body trembled. "We're surrounded up here."

Vicky heaved a weighted sigh.

"I don't think there's anything down there other than rats and darkness," Rhys said.

"Well, that makes me want to go down there more. I'd love to be surrounded by rats and darkness."

"It's better than the alternative."

After a few seconds, she shook her head. "Argh! I hope you're right." While chewing the inside of her mouth, she turned away from him and looked at the train station. "I seriously hope you're right."

So did Rhys. A quick check both ways showed it was clear. Before he could ask her if she was ready, Vicky ran at the train station at a flat-out sprint.

Chapter Twenty-Three

The metal escalator that led down to the train station had ground to a halt. As they walked down it, Rhys looked at his mismatched trainers. His and Vicky's footsteps made too much noise already, but the walk into the station in his work shoes would have sounded like a flamenco dancer had entered the building.

The escalator led into a huge underground amphitheatre. A sign hung from the ceiling in the centre of the room. It read 'Welcome to Central Station'. "I'm always overwhelmed by how grand this station is," Rhys said. His voice carried through the huge open space. "All of the others in the city are so functional. Although, it's hardly a surprise considering it's the one closest to The Alpha Tower. Everything's grandiose near that place."

Vicky didn't reply. Rhys figured she probably didn't want to talk about The Alpha Tower.

Every step reminded Rhys of how much he'd already run that day. Aches shot up through his thighs and down to his ankles as he descended with his baseball bat raised. The Rhys of ten years ago would have coped with the exercise just fine. With

Vicky a few steps behind him and seemingly managing with ease, he kept his complaints to himself.

When he turned to look back up at her, he saw that she, like him, had her bat ready for action as she searched the empty space below. There could be diseased in the shadows—not that the dumb creatures had the ability to hide; they had the subtlety of an elephant stampede.

At the bottom of the stairs, Rhys stepped off the escalator onto the white tiled floor.

Just before he headed in the direction of the platform, he turned to see Vicky had halted on the second to last step. "What's up?"

"I've got a bad feeling about this."

A quick look at their surroundings, and Rhys turned back to Vicky. "Take a look around; if there were any diseased down here, surely we'd see more evidence of them. This place is untouched."

A deep frown darkened Vicky's features.

"Besides," Rhys added, "the station is always deserted during the day. No one uses it after nine or before five. People don't come and go in Summit City. If it ain't rush hour, there isn't ever anybody down here. You know that."

"And your point is?"

"My point is what is there for the diseased to come down here for?"

She stood and stared at him, wrung her hands, and said, "I dunno what it is. I can't explain it. All I know is that I have a bad feeling… a really bad feeling."

Her anxiety put Rhys on edge. The gnawing concern in his

stomach grew sharper teeth. Not that he could tell her that, he was the one who'd suggested they came down here, so he had to keep his shit together. "Look, I understand how you feel. Considering what we've just left behind up there, none of this is going to feel good." While he held his hand out to her, he said, "Come on, trust me; this is the best way to go."

After another slight pause, Vicky took his offered hand and hopped off the bottom step. Together they walked toward the tunnel that led to the platform.

**

A buzz of something electric hid around the next corner. The urge to stop parked in Rhys' muscles, but he pushed through it. Diseased didn't sound like that, so he shouldn't worry.

But Rhys did worry, so he raised his bat as he pushed on.

When he rounded the next corner, he stopped dead. Two vending machines sat in a small alcove. Their bright lights shone in the darker tunnel.

When Vicky caught up with him, she stopped too.

"Does your card work in these ones?" he asked.

"Yep," Vicky said as she scanned the enclosed space as if the diseased could suddenly materialise from the walls.

"Can you get me a Snickers?"

Vicky frowned like she had a bad taste in her mouth. "What?"

"A Snickers; you know, a chocolate bar. I need some sustenance."

"That ain't sustenance, that's poison."

Rhys shrugged. "Fine, I need some poison then."

After she'd rolled her eyes at him, Vicky walked over to the vending machine. She swiped the card through the machine's reader then typed in a code.

Rhys' mouth watered as the machine whirred. The white metal spiral twirled and pushed the bar forward.

The bar landed in the tray at the bottom with a *thunk*. Vicky retrieved it for him and tossed it his way.

The wrapper rustled as Rhys pulled it open. It may give their position away, but he needed to eat. Also, the quicker he opened it, the less time he'd have to make the noise for. Rhys' stomach rumbled as he took a huge bite; the sickeningly sweet and chewy chocolate bar sparked life through his taste buds.

Vicky looked disgusted as she watched him. Her top lip lifted in an almost snarl and her jaw hung loose.

Not that Rhys gave a tiny shit; he needed to eat. He spoke with his mouth full. "Aren't you going to have anything?"

Vicky shook her head and wrinkled her nose more than before. "I don't eat that crap. I'll get some food later."

"Suit yourself. You're missing out though; this is good shit."

Instead of a response, Vicky stared at Rhys.

Another shrug of his shoulders and Rhys led them away from the machines.

***

The near silence held as they walked down the long tunnel that led to the platform. White glossy tiles covered both the floor and the walls. The place looked like something from the last century. Maybe that was the intention. The hard surfaces turned every footstep and rustle of the chocolate bar wrapper into an echo.

After another bite of the Snickers, Rhys looked across at Vicky. Instead of returning his glance, she continued to scan their surroundings. A bend in the tunnel up ahead obscured their view, but with the noise those things made, they'd hear them from a mile away. Especially in the echo chamber they currently occupied. "So what was it like?" Rhys asked.

For the briefest of seconds, she looked at him before she returned her focus to their surroundings. "What was what like?"

"The Alpha Tower."

Vicky didn't respond.

"Come on, Vicky; don't give me that confidential bullshit. The secret's out. Pandora's Box has been well and truly opened. Surely you can talk about it now."

The discussion seemed to cause her physical pain; tightness pinched her facial features.

Rhys took another bite of chocolate and waited.

The pair's footsteps fell in synch with one another before Vicky said, "There were a lot of secrets." She kept her focus in front of her. "Downstairs was pretty normal—grand and garish, but pretty normal. It was upstairs where everything happened. They'd turned the penthouse suite into a lab, which is where they made the virus. Everyone in the building knew about the lab, but so few of us saw it."

"Did you?"

Another deep frown, and Vicky scratched her head. "Once. About a year ago. I knew a guy who worked security. We had a thing. One night, he took me down to the room with all of the monitors—it was in the basement. I saw the labs on the screens. The guy told me what they were doing up there, but I never saw them experimenting with my own eyes."

As they continued on, about halfway down the tunnel now, Rhys said, "So where's the guy now?"

"Huh?"

"The guy in security that you were seeing?"

She looked at him with glazed eyes, but she didn't reply.

Rhys cleared the thick chocolate phlegm from his throat and the echo cannoned down the long tunnel. He didn't need to ask again. "So that was when you found out about what was happening up there?"

Vicky shook her head. "No, like I said, we all knew about it, but what could we do? If we spoke out, we'd disappear. Everyone knew that. The job paid well and they looked after you as long as you stayed on side."

A shake of his head, and Rhys spoke with another mouthful of Snickers. "How did we get to this point?"

"What do you mean?"

"Creating those fucking monsters. I mean, when the US and Europe formed a trading partnership, it seemed like a good thing, right? Who'd have guessed The East would see it as a threat and create their own?"

They got closer to the bend in the tunnel.

"All we were doing was trading," Rhys said, "but those communist nutters decided we were conspiring against them and got defensive. Another cold war based on paranoia. What's happened to the world?"

Vicky shrugged.

Rhys raised the Snickers to take another bite, but when they rounded the corner, the chocolate never made it to his mouth.

Chapter Twenty-Four

Rhys jumped backwards, crashed into Vicky, and dropped his Snickers in the process.

With her bat raised, Vicky peered around him, her breaths heavy. She finally said, "It's dead, Rhys."

The diseased lay on the floor, its head no more than battered pulp. The chocolate that Rhys had just eaten rose up in his throat. He cleared it, but an acidic burn remained. "I can see that now," he said as he stared at the last of his Snickers. It sat in the pool of blood that had spread out from the corpse. The two-second rule didn't apply here. "It looks like it's gone a few rounds with you, Vicky."

Vicky looked around without even a hint of a smile. "If there's one, there's got to be more."

"As long as they all look like this one," Rhys said, "then I don't care how many there are."

Vicky paused her search of the area and looked at Rhys.

"Anyway," Rhys said, "these things aren't the types to hang around and wait to pounce—based on what we've seen of them so far anyway. If they know there's people nearby, they're coming at you full tilt. If there's more and they're alive, we'd know about them."

"Hmm," Vicky said.

Rhys tugged on her arm. "Come on, the platform's just down here."

***

Nothing happened on the short walk to the platform. Maybe Rhys was correct about there not being any more diseased. But if he was, who'd killed it? Rhys shook his head to himself. None of that mattered right now. One foot in front of the other, deal with what came their way and nothing more. Nothing could be gained from shitting himself about a fear that may never materialise.

As Rhys looked down the long platform, he shook his head. "The last time I was here, it was rammo."

"I thought you used to drive to work?"

"Yeah, the traffic was a nightmare, but it was better than getting up close and personal with a thousand smelly commuters. It was just me and Da—" Rhys couldn't finish the sentence. Just the thought of his best mate drove a lump into his throat that choked him.

For the briefest second, Vicky looked at Rhys before she looked back to the platform.

"Do you think those locked in the towers will ever get out, Vicky?"

Although she glanced at Rhys again, Vicky didn't reply.

Grief weighed heavy in Rhys' chest and he drew a deep sigh. He then copied Vicky and searched their environment.

The distinct lack of people made it feel haunted, as if he'd just boarded a ghost ship. Being vigilant in case of the diseased was the best defence they had.

The pair walked down the rest of the platform in silence.

As they neared the end, Rhys stared into the cavernous mouth of the tunnel. Dark and ominous, it stood and waited to swallow them whole. The reluctance he'd seen from Vicky earlier suddenly spread through his own body. Nevertheless, he couldn't stop—not now.

Without breaking stride, Rhys jumped down onto the train tracks. The large stones crunched beneath his feet as he landed. For a second, he just stood there and stared into the darkness.

The expected crunch as Vicky joined him didn't come, so Rhys turned around to look up at her still on the platform. "Come on, don't think about it. Just jump down, and let's walk. Your mind will create all kinds of horrible scenarios if you let it. You'll be glad when we come out at Draw Bridge Station. Think about feeling that hot sun on your face and not seeing any of the diseased when we get there."

"But how can you know that's what'll happen?"

"I can't, but when I think about the alternatives waiting for us if we turn around…"—he shook his head—"I'd rather take my chances down here."

Another look behind, and Vicky leapt down onto the tracks to join Rhys.

After he'd rubbed her back, Rhys pulled his phone from his pocket, flicked the torch on, and shone it into the darkness. It made the next few metres easier to see, but beyond that, the deep red glow of the security lights took over.

As he stepped forward, Vicky clamped a hard grip on his arm. His pulse rocketed and he spun around to look at her. "What is it? What's wrong?"

With a shaky hand, Vicky pointed into the tunnel. "Down there, look."

Unsure as to whether he should raise his torch or bat, Rhys did both. The torch could be dropped at a moment's notice. A smashed smartphone hardly mattered if something rushed at you and tried to bite your face off.

Although Rhys swiped the torch's beam in front of them, he couldn't see anything. "What is it? What can you see?"

Vicky still shook as she pointed into the tunnel. "There. Look."

"You need to give me a bit more than that, Vicky."

Vicky's breath quickened and she jabbed her finger with more aggression at the same spot. "Down there. Rats!"

The tension of the moment left Rhys. It took everything not to laugh at her. "Fucking hell, I thought there was something serious down there. Where's the tough Vicky of only a few minutes ago? They're only rats; they can't hurt us."

"Have you seen their fucking teeth? They're nasty little bastards."

"I'd take a thousand rats over one of the diseased any fucking day. They have no interest in us, horrible yellow teeth or not."

Vicky shuddered. "Look, Rhys, I'm frightened of rats. It may not be rational, and it may be hard for you to understand, but the little shits scare the life out of me."

Rhys pushed his elbow away from his body to encourage Vicky to link arms with him. "Fear not, Fair Maiden. If you stand by my side, I will protect you from the rodent threat and make sure you return to your castle."

Although Vicky took Rhys up on his offer and slid her arm through his, she spoke with a dark tone. "Just because I'm scared of rats, doesn't mean I'm a damsel in distress. Remember who showed you how to kill the diseased in the first place. And don't forget how many times I've had to wait for you when we go for a run. It's a phobia, so don't make me feel powerless."

If the heat that rushed to his face was anything to go by, Rhys had probably glowed red at that point. Thankfully, the darkness spared his embarrassment.

Chapter Twenty-Five

After Rhys had stumbled for a second time, he turned the torch on his phone off and slipped it into his pocket. It did nothing to improve the visibility in the tunnels anyway. The red glow from the security lights, although useless for helping them see better, rendered it utterly ineffective.

The only sounds in the murky tunnel came from their own dragged footsteps and the scuttle of small creatures. Every time a rat moved, Vicky squeezed Rhys' arm. Her iron grip stung, and Rhys had to hold back his gasp. After the whole embarrassing spiel about being her protector, he could hardly moan every time she squeezed a little too tight. Besides, for the first time since he'd met her, it was nice that he could offer her comfort.

The hard walls and low roof of the tunnel amplified Rhys' whisper. "Thank you again for coming with me, Vicky. I really need your help if I'm to get to Flynn, so thank you."

Vicky watched the shadows instead of him and said, "It's okay. I figure I owe the world. All I can do is right my wrongs one person at a time. I've got to do the right thing, right?"

"Sure, but we can't change the past, and the Vicky I've met is a good person, so stop torturing yourself."

Vicky didn't reply.

"So do you have a family?"

Vicky nodded.

"One that you want to try and get to once we get out of the city?"

She shook her head with such force, it threw Rhys off balance. Then the words came fast, as if he'd broken the dam. "I was the middle child of three. I have an older and a younger brother. They're arseholes—high flyers in the city. They think the sun shines out of their own arses. They've spawned spoiled children who are as obnoxious as they are and will follow in their footsteps. Those two motherfuckers have been horrible to me forever. It was like they were put on this planet to make my life miserable."

Before Rhys could reply, she said, "Of course, it didn't help that Mum treated them like royalty. They got whatever the fuck they wanted, whenever they wanted. I got fuck all from her. She'd refer to me as 'the slut' most of the time, and they were her 'little princes'. I don't know what her problem was. I don't know why she hated me so much."

"And your dad?"

"Dead. Died when I was about three. I was always his princess; or so my brothers told me anyway. Maybe that was why Mum hated me so much. Maybe the attention he paid me made her jealous."

"And where's your mum now?"

"Also dead; she died a few years back of emphysema. She

smoked like a chimney. I cared for her for the last few years of her life and watched her ability to breathe dwindle with every passing day." She hesitated for a moment. "Is it wrong to say I didn't care?"

Rhys didn't reply. How could he comment on that?

"I hated the old cunt, Rhys. I was glad to see her go."

"So if she hated you and you hated her, why did you look after her in her final days?"

"Both of my brothers have family, and I was single. I was best placed to look after her."

"Why the fuck were you single?" Did he just say that out loud?

A coy smile broke Vicky's stern expression. After she'd brushed a strand of her curly blonde hair away from her face, she looked at Rhys. The silence hung heavy between them for a few seconds.

Rhys' heart beat harder than it had in a long time. Although he swallowed, it did little to relieve his dry throat. Vicky was beautiful. She was bright, fit, kind—

The sound of stones shifted up ahead and gatecrashed his thoughts. They both stared into the dark.

"What do you think it is?" Vicky said.

Rhys didn't reply and listened as the noise built. Within about thirty seconds, it sounded like a rush of water.

Alcoves lined either side of the tunnel. They were places for the workers to retreat into when a train came down the line. Rhys made for the one closest to them and dragged Vicky in with him. The sound grew louder. Hopefully it would go straight past them.

Chapter Twenty-Six

Rhys' heart pounded as he waited in the alcove with Vicky pressed into him. "Thank you for everything you've done," he said. "Thank you for trying to help me get to Flynn. Thank you for caring."

"It isn't over yet, Rhys."

As the sound grew louder, Vicky pressed up against him and shook. The alcove seemed like the most ridiculous place to hide. Outnumbered and overwhelmed, they didn't stand a chance against whatever the fuck came down the tunnel toward them.

Although Rhys couldn't see them, they sounded close. Suddenly, he felt something hit his foot, then something else...

After he'd rubbed his eyes, Rhys leaned out of the alcove and saw them. Rats! Hundreds of fucking rats! The scarlet glow of the security lights highlighted the undulating greasy black carpet. The horrible little fuckers filled the entire width of the tunnel.

It took Vicky a few seconds to catch up. When she inhaled hard as if to cry out Rhys clamped a hand across her mouth. As she fought against him, he whispered in her ear, "I'm sorry to do this to you, darling, but trust me."

Vicky moved her mouth against his hand as if to bite him. "Please," Rhys said, "just relax for a moment and listen to me. These rats are freaking me out too, but we have to ask what they're running from. Why are so many of them on the move? And if we make a lot of noise, will we give our position away to whatever's chasing them?"

Although she let go of her fight, she continued to shake as a sea of rats swarmed around their feet.

The rodents ran over Rhys' trainers in a constant stream. The urge to shout and kick out coursed through him, but he had to be strong. As Vicky squirmed in his grip, Rhys gently stroked her hair. "Shh, it's okay. They won't hurt you. Remember that. They won't hurt you. If I let go, can you remain silent?"

Rhys' hand moved up and down as Vicky nodded.

"Okay, I'm going to let go now, all right?"

Vicky nodded again.

Straight away, Vicky pushed her back against the wall of the alcove and placed one foot on either side of the narrow space. It lifted her about a foot from the ground, but she still seemed to be on the verge of a panic attack.

"You need to calm down," Rhys said. "Slow your breathing. Try to relax. The rats can't harm you, remember that."

As he listened to her breathing slow down, Rhys felt body after body crash into his feet and ankles. A shiver snapped through him. With so many of them on the floor, a lift of either foot and he'd have to struggle to put it back down again.

Suddenly, the squeaks and scuttles of the rats paled into insignificance as Rhys heard it. Deeper sounds echoed down the tunnel—heavy breaths, thick and phlegmy; irregular footsteps that stumbled and tripped; the smack of wet jaws followed by low growls.

Vicky adjusted her feet next to him and the sound of the soles of her shoes scraped the walls. Rhys tried to control his own panic, which swelled through his chest. With his baseball bat raised, he waited.

Chapter Twenty-Seven

The smell hit Rhys well before he caught sight of it. Rotten meat combined with rancid vinegar. It forced his tongue to the roof of his mouth and flipped his stomach. Tense from trying to prevent himself from vomiting, Rhys waited for the thing to appear.

When the last of the rats passed them, Rhys held his breath and stared into the darkness.

A few seconds later, the thing that had spooked the rats came around the corner. It moved with a lurching gait as it almost tripped over its own clumsiness. For some reason, this one moved with more trouble than the ones they'd encountered so far. It looked like it carried an injury.

The glow of one of the red lights caught the thing's face and Rhys flinched. He suddenly understood the reason for the wet squelch. He winced as the thing took another bite into the headless rat like it was a turkey drumstick. It seemed to sate its hunger, which in turn seemed to dull its sense for prey.

The creature stared straight ahead as it walked, uninterested in its surroundings as it took yet another bite on the rat. No doubt, it'd be back to high alert when the rat ran out.

With the thing just a few metres away from them, Rhys backed farther into the alcove. He pressed into Vicky, who continued to tremble against him. Suddenly she slipped. The scratch of her shoe against the dry brick wall stopped the diseased dead in its tracks. It dropped the rat and its jaw spread wide.

Before it could roar, Rhys stepped forward and swung his bat. It connected with the side of the diseased's head and knocked it to the ground. Vicky appeared next to him and crushed its skull with one brutal swing.

Both Rhys and Vicky stared at one another then looked down the tunnel in the direction the diseased and the rats had come from. Rhys looked back down at the fallen diseased before he said, "We need to get the fuck out of here. Now."

Vicky nodded.

The pair moved at a fast walk. Both of them kept their bats raised. The dark red glow of their surroundings revealed nothing to Rhys other than deep shadows and the vividness of his own imagination.

"How much longer until Draw Bridge Station, Rhys?"

Too long. "I don't know," he said. Why had he taken them down there?

Clumsy because of their inability to see, both Rhys and Vicky kicked stones away from them every few steps. So strung out, Rhys jumped every single time it happened.

"I don't know if it's better having walls on either side or worse," Vicky said. "I mean, we can see there's nothing hiding around us, but we've got nowhere to run to."

"We'll be fine. Just keep going." The warble in Rhys' voice did little to back up his assertion. Good job she couldn't hear his rapid heartbeat too.

The pair picked the pace up another notch as they grew more comfortable on the uneven ground. Then Rhys snagged his foot.

Everything moved in slow motion as he fell forward. Halfway down, he let go of his bat and it clattered against the floor with several loud pings. The sharp stones crunched as they cut into his knees and hands. Despite the burn, he held his breath and listened. If there were more diseased, they now knew Rhys and Vicky were there.

About a minute of silence passed before Rhys got to his feet again. Vicky stared at him, wide-eyed and frozen to the spot. "Come on," he said, "let's keep moving."

Sweat stung the cuts on Rhys' palms as he held the bat. His bruised kneecaps forced him to walk with a slight limp, but he pushed on. When they rounded the next corner, they both stopped again.

They could see the end of the tunnel.

Chapter Twenty-Eight

After he'd jumped up onto the platform, Rhys reached down to Vicky. He took her soft hand and pulled her up. He held on for a second longer than he had to.

When he'd finally let go of her, Rhys dusted himself down and looked around. "There's a lot more nooks and crannies here than at Central Station. More places to hide." His voice, although soft, carried along the quiet platform.

He listened to Vicky's quick breaths as she looked around too. She finally said, "I don't like it, Rhys. I don't like it one little bit."

"Me neither."

As in the tunnel, Rhys gripped his bat and walked down the platform with Vicky by his side. Pain ran through his kneecaps like hot irons had been wedged into them. Other than an involuntary grimace, he didn't let it get the better of him.

Pillars, each one about a metre thick, ran the length of Draw Bridge Station. They ran from floor to ceiling, and no matter how Rhys craned his neck, he couldn't see the entire platform all at once at any one time.

"Anything could be hiding down here," Vicky said.

Rhys took a deep breath to keep his voice even and try to settle the Snickers, which churned in his knotted stomach. "We just need to keep going. We'll hear them before they get to us." He then added, "I hope."

Vicky released a strained sigh.

With some of the lights out on the platform, the shadows became too dark to see into. Anything could be hiding in them and waiting to jump out. Rhys had already told Vicky that wouldn't happen, and it wouldn't—the diseased were full tilt; they didn't do stealth. But it didn't stop him squinting to see into the shadows. His eyes stung as he searched the darkness.

To exit the platform, they had to climb an enclosed spiral staircase. Brown tiled walls and terracotta steps didn't help when coupled with the poor light.

Halfway up the staircase, a bright bulb flickered. The pair stopped as one.

The light buzzed while it strobed. Rhys listened out for the call of the diseased.

Nothing.

When he put a hand on Vicky's shoulder, she jumped. He waited for her to face him. "Are you ready to move again?"

At first, she didn't reply, but then she nodded. They resumed their ascent and the sound of their footsteps raced up the stairs ahead of them.

"They're going to hear us, Rhys."

"We have to keep going," Rhys said. "If they hear us, we fight."

Although Rhys kept his attention in front of him, he saw

Vicky wring her grip on her baseball bat in his peripheral vision. "I'm ready if they come," she said.

The stairs came out into an open area, similar to the one in Central Station but much smaller. It seemed clear.

Like Central Station, this place had escalators that ran in and out of the main entrance. Like Central Station, they'd stopped working.

The clang of their feet on the metal stairs called out, and Rhys resisted the urge to run. To arrive at the drawbridge knackered wouldn't serve anybody.

***

When Rhys stepped out of Draw Bridge Station, the sun blinded him. He dug his fists into his eyes and his heart raced. Those things could be surrounding them, for all he knew. Baseball bat or not, he'd have to swing blind.

Although the tunnel had felt stuffy and oppressive, being outside again made the thick summer heat push against Rhys' skin like a heavy blanket in a sauna. Sweat rose on his brow and ran into his eyes.

It seemed to take a lifetime to get his sight back, and he'd rubbed his eyes so hard they hurt. When he could finally see again, he scanned around. A wide road ran alongside Draw Bridge Station. Rhys had a clear line of sight both up and down it that allowed him to see there were no diseased.

The alleyway to the drawbridge was on the other side of the road, sandwiched between two towers. Rhys couldn't remember the numbers for the buildings, but what did it matter? They all looked the same. When he looked at Vicky, he smiled. "See, I told you going through the tunnel was a good plan."

Darkness sat in Vicky's azure eyes and thick bags rested beneath them. She acknowledged his comment with a nod. "It worked. That's all I'm giving you." A half smile lifted the side of her mouth. "If I'd have known what we were to go through down there, I think I would have joined the school trip to The Alpha Tower."

Rhys winced.

"Too soon for those jokes?"

Rhys nodded.

"My point still stands. You have a cute kid, but don't ever ask me to do that again for him, because I will say no."

Rhys reached across and squeezed her forearm. "Thank you."

Although Vicky didn't reply, some of the darkness left her eyes.

"I didn't notice any infected rats down there, did you?" Rhys said.

"Ew! Why would you even put that thought in my head?"

"What I mean is I think the virus only affects human beings."

Vicky hugged herself as if for warmth. "Let's hope so; I fucking hate the idea of a mass of infected rodents… of any creature, for that matter."

Rhys nodded across the road to the alley that led to the drawbridge. "You ready to go?"

After another look around, Vicky said, "Yep, let's do it."

***

They got to the end of the alley and Rhys stopped. Intuition, fear, or some other deep instinct told him to halt. He raised a palm at Vicky for her to stay where she was and peered out at the drawbridge. His stomach sank to his bollocks. "Oh fuck!"

It was a struggle to hold onto his rapid breaths, let alone explain to Vicky what he'd just seen, so Rhys pulled back into the alleyway and let Vicky look past him.

The colour drained from her beautiful face and she quickly pulled herself back in again. She ran her hand over the top of her head to pull her hair away from her eyes and said, "Shit!"

When the initial spike of panic settled, Rhys looked out again. About twenty metres of road separated them and the entrance to the drawbridge—a short run at best, but they wouldn't be able to do much when they got there. Blue flashing lights pulsed on the other side of the river behind a temporarily erected police blockade. At least ten feet tall and as wide as the bridge, it was made from toughened plastic. It had been erected to stop anything getting out of the city, including Vicky and Rhys. It currently had a herd of diseased pressed up against it. They could evidently smell prey but had no idea of how to get to them.

Rhys jumped when Vicky spoke. "How the fuck are we to get through that lot?"

Gargles, groans, and the occasional frustrated yell filled the air. "Why have we got this stupid fucking arms embargo?" Rhys said. "All countries gave up their weapons! For what? It doesn't make any fucking sense! How could a handgun in England harm someone in China? If the police had guns, we'd be home free by now."

Rhys turned to Vicky and his voice wavered when he said, "How the fuck are we going to get across, Vick? How the fuck am I going to get to my boy?"

Chapter Twenty-Nine

Inaction gripped Rhys' muscles as he stood at the mouth of the alleyway. If he stepped out, the diseased would see him and tear him apart in seconds. "Fuck it," he said again.

"Fuck it ain't going to give us a solution, honey."

"How can we have come so far to get screwed at the last minute? 'Fuck it' is all I have."

"It still won't fix anything."

Heat rushed beneath Rhys' skin, and he balled his fists. "So what do you have to offer? Maybe if you stopped criticising me and came up with something useful… If it was your son…" his words trailed off when he looked at her, her eyes wide, her head pulled back. "I'm sorry," he said, "it's not your fault. You're right; 'fuck it' isn't an answer to anything. So how are we going to get across that bridge? There are hundreds of them." Rhys watched the steady stream of diseased that joined the already dense crowd. "How much longer will that police blockade last before they get through?"

Vicky placed her baseball bat against the wall and looked back at Rhys. A sense of calm rested in her eyes that he hadn't seen from her before. Her usual hostility had abated. "The opportunity is going to come. It's important that you make the most of it when it does, and think only of your boy, yeah?"

"What are you—?"

"Just think about Flynn, okay?"

Rhys nodded, and before he could say anything else to her, Vicky sprinted out from the alleyway.

Chapter Thirty

Rhys shook his head as he watched Vicky run away from him. She'd abandoned him. A few words of encouragement, and then so long, partner, it's been emotional, but fuck you and fuck your helpless fucking son. What a bitch!

With her name on his tongue, it took everything Rhys had not to call after her. It wouldn't do any good. The diseased didn't understand words; they just understood noise and honed in on it. He wouldn't last two seconds if he shouted his mouth off.

Vicky moved fast. Suddenly Rhys saw just how much he'd slowed her down. No wonder she'd chosen to leave. She had to be alone to survive, but it made no sense to run back into the city.

Then she screamed. "Oi, fuckos, I'm over here. Fresh meat if you want it, fuck nuts."

Rhys' chin damn near hit the ground and he shook his head again. She couldn't outrun them. Not that many. No fucking way.

The diseased didn't react at first. Instead, they continued to push against the temporary barrier, but then she called out again and Rhys saw one of them at the back turn around to look at her. As dense as the rest, it had a deep wound that ran down the side of its face and blood streaked its cheeks. Then something akin to clarity spread across its features.

When it screamed, its entire upper body bounced up and down. It looked like it used its own body weight to pump the deep cry from its lungs. The pack responded. It started with those close to it but soon spread through the entire mob.

The assault on the police barricade stopped, and as one, the diseased took off after her.

Despite the distance and chaotic mob between them, Rhys still heard her clearly. "That's it, you stupid bastards. Come on, follow me."

As the diseased left the bridge, Rhys' heart galloped to the point where he struggled to breathe. She'd given him the opportunity to escape and rescue Flynn. The burn of tears itched his eyeballs. She should have told him before she did it. He wouldn't have let her go; she knew that as much as he did.

Rhys picked up Vicky's bat, rubbed his eyes, cleared the lump from his throat, and headed over to the now empty bridge.

When he got close, the sickly sweet funk of death floated in the air. The sheer density of the crowd had turned the atmosphere sour, even after they'd gone.

But before he stepped onto the bridge, Rhys watched Vicky, the thunderous call of hundreds of clumsy feet on her trail. He had a clear view of her from his elevated position. She ran straight for a small florist's shop. Of course... her card.

A loud *crash* sounded as Vicky collided with the shutter at the front of the shop. Even from this distance, Rhys saw the flash of her white card as she swiped it through the florist's reader. The metal shutter lifted—slowly; too fucking slowly.

While he chewed on his bottom lip, Rhys watched the shutter and then the gap between Vicky and the diseased. They were gaining on her. She didn't have the time to wait for it, but she waited anyway. She divided her attention between the mob behind, and the barrier as it slowly rose.

As the diseased got closer, each one loosed its own scream at the sky.

Vicky paced up and down and kept her eyes on the diseased. Surely she would run. It was the worst game of chicken ever. Rhys would have shit himself by now and bottled it. Not that Rhys would have put himself in that situation in the first place. She was a hero. She'd sacrificed herself for a photo and a sob story.

The shutter continued to rise, and Vicky held her ground.

When the gap grew large enough, Vicky dropped to her front and dragged herself under. Her entire upper body disappeared, but her legs still hung out when the first creature hit the shutter with a loud *crash*.

Several more clattered into it. One of the leaders grabbed at Vicky's foot, but she kicked out and managed to pull herself under and out of sight.

Then the shutter stopped.

It dropped again.

She must have swiped the reader inside.

Some of the diseased dropped to the ground and tried to follow Vicky under.

Because the gap tightened, only a few of them actually attempted it. The rest bashed against the metal.

A couple of diseased made it into the shop. It could have been worse, but that didn't untie the knots of anxiety in Rhys' stomach. It would only take one to kill her. The weight of Vicky's baseball bat sat in Rhys' grip; he hoped she'd find something in the shop to use against them.

The third diseased that tried to get through had been pinned to the ground by the barrier as it closed. It screamed as it pressed down on its back. The diseased equivalent of a bleating lamb; panic and fury combined in its shrill and repetitive caw. It seemed to disturb the other diseased so much they backed away. It afforded Rhys the clearest view of the thing.

When the shutter pushed into the diseased's clothes at the base of its spine, it cried louder than before and kicked its legs. The upper half of its body had made it into the shop.

A deep *crack*, and its legs fell limp, but the thing still screamed.

Then it stopped. Vicky must have killed it.

One of the creatures at the front of the pack yelled. The fury spread through the mob again and they rushed forward as one.

A loud crash sounded out as they bashed against the steel shutter again and again.

Chapter Thirty-One

The bright sun stung Rhys' eyes as he stood by the bridge and watched the shopfront get battered. A pain tore through his chest. There had to be a way to get Vicky out of there, but how?

"If you want to come, now's the time."

Rhys turned to see an officer at the end of the bridge. He'd opened a gap in the barricade and motioned for Rhys to come through.

Red-faced as he scanned around wildly, his hand gestures grew more animated. "Are you deaf or something? If you want to get out of this place, now's the time."

The crowd of diseased outside the florist had thickened to the point where Rhys couldn't see the shutter anymore. The mass of crazed and frantic lunatics made it look like hell had opened up into Summit City, and Vicky was at the centre of it.

When Rhys looked back, the officer had halved the distance between them. An older man with white hair, he looked like he'd waited patiently for retirement. A couple of years left in the job and then he could get away and start to live his life. Softness radiated from him that Rhys rarely saw in younger officers. The need to nick people had clearly been well and truly played out for him.

"Come on, lad," he said. "Come over the bridge with me, and make that girl's life mean something."

She didn't have to lose her life so he could rescue his son; there had to be a way for both of them to come through this.

When the police officer touched Rhys on the shoulder, Rhys jumped away.

"Steady on, son." The officer spoke as if he was talking to a jittery horse. He tugged on Rhys' arm. "We're raising this drawbridge. If you don't come with us now, we're going to have to leave you."

Several officers watched the interaction from the other side of the barricade. Rhys turned back to the florist's and his heart lifted when he saw Vicky on the roof.

When she waved her arms, he smiled. "She's alive."

"That's all well and good," the cop said, "but those monsters are persistent fuckers, and they ain't going anywhere until they get to her."

Then, over the groans and wails, Rhys heard her faint voice. "Go and get Flynn; I'll be fine."

Rhys looked at Vicky for a few seconds longer before he turned to the officer. "Can you do one thing for me?"

The officer's eyes narrowed, but he didn't say anything.

"Do you know St. Michael's Primary School?"

"Yes," the officer said.

"Can you go and check that it's okay? My boy's there."

The officer's entire frame sank. "You're not coming?"

The florist's stood in the shadow of two tall buildings—if

they could even be called buildings; skeletons seemed like a more appropriate word for their semi-constructed state. While he stared at them, Rhys replied to the officer. "I am coming, just not yet. I can't leave her; it's not right. Will you please go to the school for me?"

After a slight pause, the officer said, "Yes."

Like Vicky had done earlier, Rhys rested both his bat and hers against the bridge. He then patted the older officer's shoulder. "Thank you; I'll be ten minutes behind you."

Rhys then took off down the hill towards the herd of the diseased and the shop with Vicky inside.

Chapter Thirty-Two

Although Rhys followed the same path Vicky had originally taken, to continue along that line of trajectory would have landed him smack bang in the middle of the herd. His plan had more smarts than that.

The vinegary stink of rot hit Rhys sooner than he'd expected. In just a few hours, the diseased smelled like their flesh had curdled. At this rate, they'd be nothing but piles of sludge in a few days. Whatever happened to them over time, Rhys wouldn't be there to find out—no fucking way; he, Vicky, and Flynn would be long gone.

With about twenty metres between Rhys and the stragglers at the back of the pack, Rhys changed his course and headed for a small building.

One of seven small huts was positioned off to the side. They'd all gone into lockdown like the other buildings in Summit City, but when they didn't have armour around them, they served a variety of food to the Summit City workers. Now they served as a way for Rhys to hide from the diseased crowd.

A dull ache gripped Rhys' lower back as he tried to run at a crouch. He stopped when he got to the first hut. Each hut stood about three metres tall; he didn't need to run like that. Crouched or not, the diseased couldn't see him. With two hands on the base of his back, he leaned backwards and thrust his pelvis out as he released a muted groan.

After his slight pause, Rhys moved along to the next hut on tiptoes. As he ran, he listened to the collective moans and roars on the other side of the small buildings. If he couldn't see them, they couldn't see him. Although… if he couldn't see them, he also couldn't see an attack. There could be a welcoming party past hut number seven and he'd know fuck all about it.

A sharp ache ran through his feet and he fell from his tiptoed run, but he carried on.

Suddenly, Rhys heard something else and stopped. Muffled and distant, he heard it nonetheless—a small voice whimpered and cried. A stream of sweat ran down the sides of Rhys' face as he searched around for the source of the sound.

When he leaned against the steel panel of the closest food hut, he instantly withdrew from the hot metal shutters. It must have been scorching inside… Inside! The thick steel made it almost impossible to hear the person, but the voice came from inside the hut. Rhys moved his face so close, he felt the heat that radiated from the brushed metal.

"Help me, please. Help me."

He couldn't do anything. The thick reinforced steel barely let sound through, so any effort Rhys made to help the woman inside would be utterly ineffective. Even if he could help her, the noise he'd have to make would bring the diseased over in droves.

A woman trapped as she cried for help twisted a pang of grief through Rhys' chest, but he couldn't help her. Vicky remained the number one priority at that moment. Get Vicky, get Flynn, and then get as far away as possible—nothing else mattered. Rhys stepped away a couple of paces and frowned at the steel pod. A lump rose in his throat. Poor woman. When he looked up at the sun, he squinted and shook his head. She'd probably die in there like a dog left in a hot car.

Three heavy clunks and then a whirring sound took Rhys' attention away from the food pod. He looked across to see the drawbridge as it slowly lifted. Fear gripped him; no going back now. A look at the two half-built towers flooded him with self-doubt. Rhys took a deep breath and whispered to himself, "One thing at a time." It did little to calm his furious pulse.

***

It took a few minutes for the bridge to lift. Without a friendly cop on the other side, it had become impassable. Whether Rhys had made the correct choice to go back for Vicky didn't matter anymore. It now remained his only choice.

The noise of the bridge had pulled some of the diseased back over. They shambled, rather than ran, toward it; curiosity drove them rather than hunger. They seemed to understand the disturbance wouldn't provide them with something to hunt. It must be an olfactory thing; the drawbridge, although no doubt had a metallic quality to it, didn't reek of human blood.

The crowd that headed to the bridge consisted of maybe fifteen diseased at most. The ones that banged against the florist's steel shutter continued to hammer away; they undoubtedly still believed they could get into the shop.

Once Rhys arrived at the end of the line of food pods, he peered at the tall, unfinished buildings that were much closer now. He saw straight through them because neither of them had doors or windows fitted yet. They'd best be as barren inside. In fact, his entire plan relied on it.

The heat of the day and Rhys' anxiety had turned his mouth dry. He took a deep breath and counted down from three before he poked his head around to look at the diseased.

The second he did, his heart jolted and rattled his nerves.

He was being watched.

Chapter Thirty-Three

If he waved at her, it would attract their attention. Instead, Rhys held eye contact with Vicky, and with a very slow gesture, pointed at the tall buildings just across the way.

For a few seconds, she looked at the half-built towers. When she looked back, she nodded at Rhys, gave him the thumbs up, and disappeared from the roof of the florist's.

The sound of the diseased as they crashed against the steel grew louder. Something had evidently wound them up.

From where Rhys stood, nothing had changed with the shop. Maybe the diseased farther back had redoubled their efforts to get forward, but even that didn't explain the extra noise.

Unless… "Vicky," Rhys whispered. When he strained his ears, he heard it. Some of the bangs came from the other side of the shutter. It pulled the diseased in, and their collective intention bore down harder on the steel barrier that stood between them and Vicky. However, regardless of how hard they pushed, the barrier held.

When their moans and cries grew louder still, Rhys muttered

to himself, "Good girl, Vicky." His opportunity had arrived.

A slight reluctance gripped Rhys' muscles, and it nearly held him back. Then he shook his head. Not now. Not when Vicky needed him. Rhys took a final breath and sprinted out into the open space.

Once he was out of cover, he glanced across at the rowdy mob. If one of them saw him now... well, it didn't bear thinking about.

Yet, not a single creature turned to look at him; Vicky had them well and truly occupied.

***

Rhys darted into the unfinished building and pressed his back against an inside wall. Surrounded by bare concrete, it threw back an echo of not only his footsteps, but also his hard breaths.

The place had a long way to go before completion. Most of the large rooms were yet to have their dividing walls erected. Dust from the construction tickled Rhys' nose, but he managed to hold onto his sneeze.

In an attempt to cool himself down, Rhys pulled his shirt away from his stomach and billowed it like a fan. Although the cheap nylon didn't cater to this kind of heat nor this kind of exercise, he could hardly go skins—not a great way to impress Vicky. A beautiful and fit young woman nearly ten years his junior could hardly be attracted to Rhys, a slightly portly thirty-something bloke whose best physical attributes were his calf muscles because they kept his odd-shaped body stable.

The bare concrete stairs ran a spiral all the way to the top of the building. It made Rhys dizzy to look up the centre of them.

More dust ran up Rhys' nose, and his eyes watered. A sneeze stirred in his nostrils, but with a hard rub of his face and a sharp sniff, it passed. He didn't need to attract those things too early. If he did, he wouldn't be able to outrun them up what must have been at least twenty flights of stairs.

A final deep breath, and he began his climb.

***

Tools lay strewn about the floor, dropped where workers left them. This place had been abandoned in a hurry. When the explosion sounded out and the shutters went up, if they had any sense, the builders would have gotten off the island in a flash. He hoped they'd made it, but it was doubtful. It would only be a matter of time before Rhys figured he'd see a diseased in a high-visibility vest. Good job they left the tools behind; they hardly needed to be armed as well.

***

By the time he'd made it up five flights of stairs, Rhys' lungs had tightened to the point where he couldn't carry on. Sweat stung his eyes as he stopped to rest, and the dusty environment made his throat dry.

Rhys pulled the photo of Flynn from his top pocket. The photographer had asked his boy to lean forwards on the table in front of him—a very adult pose for a little boy. The slightest smile tickled Rhys' lips and he kissed it. "Not long now, mate. Daddy's coming."

With that, he carried on.

***

By floor ten, Rhys paused again. Although he remained on his feet, he hunched over, placed his hands just above his knees, and fought for breath. While he stared at the floor, he watched his sweat land on the dusty ground and form dark little circles.

The need to sneeze returned, the fine dust in the air impossible to avoid. It danced in a nearby beam of light and made his eyes itch.

When a loud shriek flew into the building, Rhys stood up straight and peered down the centre of the stairs. Nothing had entered yet; he had to keep on going.

Rhys moved off again. Every step set a fire beneath his kneecaps. If they came in now, he couldn't outrun them to the top.

As he climbed, Rhys heard another shriek and looked down through the stairs again. Time seemed to stop at that moment. Shame it hadn't stopped a few seconds before—or, more precisely, *he* hadn't stopped. If he had, he would have had a second to catch his breath. If he'd have stopped, he would have realised that, although unmistakably close outside, nothing was on his trail. If he'd have stopped, he would have seen the tray of paints before he stepped on them.

Half of the paint tray hung over the edge of one of the steps as if put there as a trap. When Rhys' foot made the slightest contact with it, it nudged it off the edge. Dread sank through Rhys as the tray, and six large paint cans, fell to the ground.

They tumbled in silence and the entire world seemed to hold its breath with Rhys.

The first can connected with a stair with a loud *crash*.

Rhys' entire being tensed up to the point where he felt brittle. The next five cans shattered him as they hit the floor, almost as one. A deep *boom* shot up the stairwell. A large cloud of dust kicked up from the point of impact

And then silence…

Unable to still his heavy heartbeat, Rhys held his breath and listened.

Nothing.

Nothing inside, but nothing outside either; no bang of fists against the steel shutter at the front of the florist, no moans from the mindless mass, no shuffle of tired feet. In a world were chaos reigned, everything had turned deathly still.

Then he saw it: one diseased man. At a guess, Rhys would have put the guy in his forties. For a moment, he looked at the paints on the floor as if they would provide answers for him. Then he looked up and his bloody eyes stared straight at Rhys.

"Fuck it."

When he drew a deep breath, Rhys took off, his legs on fire from the effort.

The primitive and frenzied call of the diseased chased up the building after him.

Chapter Thirty-Four

Every part of Rhys' body ached as he pushed on. If what he'd heard about a wall was true, he'd fucking hit it. Although, a wall sounded surmountable... he'd hit six-foot thick steel. He gritted his teeth and kept going. Wall or not, he had hundreds of fucking diseased on his tail. Two options sat before him: run or die.

The thunder of footsteps pounded against the stairs behind Rhys. It turned from a military march, into a drumroll, into a continuous vibration that ran through the core of the building. It seemed like the entire place could collapse beneath their collective weight, especially as the tower could be structurally unsound in its incomplete state. Rhys shook his head to himself; it didn't help to think like that, he had to push on.

When Rhys looked down at the line of diseased that had entered the building, his stomach lurched. What little strength he had left in his legs nearly abandoned him. Packed so tightly together, they became a single unending entity with one thing on its mind—him.

Rhys looked up again. To look behind served no purpose;

the rumble of the stampede told him everything he needed to know—*keep fucking running.*

Two more flights of stairs until the roof. Like the car park, he had to get to the gap and jump. If he could get up there, he could make the jump. If he'd done it once…

When he rounded the next bend, Rhys saw the access to the roof and nearly puked. It had a fucking door on it. Of all the places in the building to have fitted a door!

Without breaking stride, Rhys crashed into it as he snapped the handle down. The impact stung and the door didn't budge.

Exhaustion, fear, and grief combined as he released a throat-splitting scream. "Arghhhhhhhh!"

If the door didn't open, the only way to avoid the inevitable would be to take the plunge down the gap in the middle of the stairs. The way of the paint cans had to be better than what these creatures would do to him.

With just two flights of stairs between him and the leaders of the pack, Rhys' breath grew shallow and pains tore through his chest.

The diseased showed no signs of fatigue.

For a moment, Rhys froze, transfixed as he watched the casualties of the crowded ascent. With no railings to stop them, the diseased that weren't firmly on the stairs fell down the gap in the middle. Their fellow monsters watched them, and some even reached out as if to catch them, but none of them stopped in their push to get to Rhys.

The collection of broken bodies at the bottom of the stairs increased by the second; maybe Rhys should jump… at least a soft landing waited for him. He turned back to look at the door.

There had to be a way through.

A small cupboard sat just next to the locked door. It reminded Rhys of the kind of place used to keep the janitor's equipment, but it didn't have a door—of course it didn't; there was only one door in this building. A bag of tools lay on the floor in the corner of the cupboard. There had to be something he could use in there.

The thick bag made a *whoosh* and kicked up a cloud of dust as Rhys dragged it toward him. When he unzipped it, he gasped. A sledgehammer lay on top of all the other tools like it had been left there for him.

Rhys jumped to his feet and swung it at the centre of the door with a yell. The heavy head sank into the wood, but the door didn't give. Hardly a surprise—he'd just hit the centre of the fucking door.

Locked in a battle with his shaky limbs, Rhys yanked the handle up and down to wriggle the hammer free.

One final tug and it came loose. It hung from his grip as Rhys turned and looked behind him—bleeding eyes fixed on him as they rounded the final bend in the staircase.

A surge of adrenaline rushed through him and he swung at the door again. He smashed the handle off and the door flew wide to the groan of splintering wood.

Before he made a run for it, Rhys turned to the pack. A tidal wave of disease and hate rushed up at him. He wound the hammer back and swung it with all his strength.

The head of the hammer connected under the chin of the lead infected like an uppercut. The force lifted it clean off its feet and sent it back into the pack. More spilled over and fell down the stairwell, and their bodies bounced off the jagged concrete steps. Each impact seemed to break them a little more until the damaged forms hit the ground like sacks of grain.

Before Rhys ran, the creatures did something that made him pause.

The pack of diseased had gathered around the one Rhys had just attacked. They held their dead friend tight and stared at Rhys. As one, they snarled and bit at the air. They hadn't paused because they were scared about what he could do to them; they'd paused because they were angry. He'd hurt one of their own.

Rhys' skin crawled as he yelled and threw the hammer at the mob. They screamed louder than before, cast their recently killed member aside, and gave chase again.

With no more than a few metres lead on the pack, Rhys ran. He gritted his teeth and his heart boomed.

The hot sun beamed down as he sprinted across the roof. The ragged breaths of the diseased in the lead got so close they damn near tickled the back of his neck. He could taste their stale aroma.

When he got to the edge of the roof, doubt grabbed him in a strangle hold, but he pushed through it and jumped anyway.

Chapter Thirty-Five

Rhys stumbled but didn't fall when he landed on the other side. He stopped and turned around to see the lead diseased continue to run straight off the edge of the building. It didn't even try to jump.

A few seconds later, Rhys heard a faint *thump* as it hit the ground below. Another one, despite some last-minute attempts to slow down, didn't manage it in time either and followed the first over the edge. The rest stopped then snarled and hissed while they focused on Rhys.

The hot sun beat down on Rhys as he caught his breath. He watched the diseased across the metre and a half of empty space that separated the two buildings. Most of them could jump it if they put their minds to it. But therein lay the problem; they didn't have minds, at least not ones that could perform any kind of function other than run and attack.

Rhys hawked up a ball of phlegm. It tasted stale in his dry mouth. He stepped close to the edge and spat across at them. It missed, but despite their obvious lack of mental function, it did something to incite them further. After he'd shown them the back of his middle finger, Rhys said, "Fuck you," and left the roof.

The second building had no door to block access to the roof. Once Rhys entered it, the dust clogged his sinuses and he sneezed. When he looked down the spiral concrete staircase, his stomach lurched and his head spun. Without any railings to hold onto, the prospect of a quick descent daunted him much more than the effort of running up them had.

At the bottom of the second flight of stairs, tiredness got the better of him. He stumbled and fell into the opposite wall. He paused for a moment and panted as he listened to the groans and moans from the top of the first tower. He had to get up and keep going.

***

When Rhys got to the bottom of the second tower, he paused and leaned against a wall. Despite deep breaths, he couldn't get enough oxygen into his body, but he couldn't hang around either.

Rhys poked his head outside and glanced up at the top of the first tower. The bright sun stung his eyes, but he continued to look up the tall building. Without the motivation of the crazed mob behind him, there was no way he would have jumped a gap that high from the ground. As a kid, he always avoided the free-running clubs—hell, he didn't even climb ladders if he didn't have to.

The diseased continued to gather at the top and reach across the gap exactly as they had done on the car park. The stupid bastards clearly thought he would reappear at some point—long may that continue. If those things had brains too, they would be the ultimate killing machines. The fact they had empathy for one another gave him chills.

The sound of rapid footsteps forced Rhys back inside the second tower and into the shadows. Seconds later, two more slathering, slobbering, diseased ex-humans shot straight into the entrance of the first building and disappeared up the stairs. The entire building shook from the sheer weight of numbers that continued to run up it. If only the structure would collapse now.

Rhys didn't know how much time he had. The diseased could spend the next day at the top of the first tower as they waited for him to reappear. On the other hand, they could work it out in five minutes and Summit City would be awash with them again.

Rhys' heart damn near exploded, and he jumped backwards when a loud *thud* hit the ground nearby. A shake took a hold of him when he poked his head around the corner to find the broken body of a diseased. Next to the couple that fell from the roof earlier, it lay motionless save for its bloody eyes that rolled in its head before they looked straight at Rhys. Fury and frustration glared at him in equal measure, but thankfully, its voice didn't work.

Another one hit the ground and kicked up a cloud of dust. The impact killed it immediately. A glance up at the top of the first tower, and Rhys saw the problem.

Thud!

Another one hit the ground. A woman this time.

The pack at the top of the first tower continued to reach across the gap as they had done at the car park. However, with the first tower still shaking from the sheer weight of diseased that ran up it, space seemed to run out up there. Every few seconds a new one fell.

Thud!

A small girl.

Thud!

An old man.

Thud!

A young woman.

It was like watching the coin machines at the fair with the drawers that moved.

Thud!

If one had landed and still had the use of its eyes, it may not be long before one still had the use of its voice.

Thud!

On high alert, Rhys stepped away from the bodies and toward the florist's shop. He had to go now.

***

To stay out of the line of sight of the diseased on the roof, Rhys ran close to a wall that led most of the way there.

Once he got to the first corner, he peered around it. Nothing; it seemed that every single one of diseased in the area had run up the tower.

He chanced another look back at the first tower and watched them continue to reach across the gap between the two buildings. They continued to fall.

"Stupid bastards," Rhys said. Although, all it took was for one of them to see him… he never wanted to hear one of those fuckers scream again. A chill snapped through him at the thought of that sound. He needed to get to Flynn now.

Rhys looked around the corner toward the florist's one final time. The coast seemed clear. A quick knock on the shutter and Vicky would open up. Then they could get out of there. He'd heard the person in the food booth, so surely Vicky would hear him.

Three, two, one. Rhys took off around the corner and stopped dead instantly. The wind left his body and his jaw hung loose as he stared.

The shutter had already been opened. The empty shop had been painted red with blood.

Chapter Thirty-Six

The walls, the floor, the doorway that lead to the roof… blood covered the lot. There had been a struggle and someone had most definitely lost.

When Rhys poked his head inside, he balked at the mix of a metallic tang of fresh blood and the diseased reek of rot. Then he saw it… her.

Face down on the floor, in an ever-increasing pool of her own blood, he saw Vicky. Her blonde curls splayed away from her in a twisted halo that stretched out like the intertwined roots of a tree. The thick blood stood in stark contrast to her fair hair.

A lump rose in his throat. She'd only had to wait and he would have been there. She must have opened the shutter too early.

Another look at the top of the first undeveloped tower showed the roof still crammed with the diseased, and Rhys' vision blurred.

Rhys had to go. One last look at Vicky, and his lip buckled. Warm tears ran down his cheeks. A wet sniff, and he wiped his nose with the back of his sleeve. Then he took off in the direction of the drawbridge.

***

Grief and exhaustion turned Rhys' legs bandy as he ran. He should have told Vicky how he felt about her. Although 'should haves' didn't get him anywhere. Besides, grieving wasn't an option at that moment; he had to get to his son. Nothing had changed in that respect.

With the diseased still crammed on the roof of the first tower, Rhys took the most direct line to the bridge. The open space he had to run across left him in plain sight of the diseased, but he needed to get off the island immediately.

As he ran, he cried. Without breaking stride, he wiped his streaming eyes and pushed on. When he and Flynn were safe, he could deal with his emotions about Vicky. Until then, he had to keep going.

***

When Rhys arrived at the bridge, exhausted and out of breath, he saw the baseball bats had vanished. "What the hell?" He did a quick scan of his surroundings but couldn't see them anywhere.

Tension crawled up his back and held on. It didn't matter what he told himself, he couldn't avoid the obvious conclusion—the disappearance of the bats had nothing to do with the diseased; someone had taken them. Yet he couldn't see anyone around, so whoever had taken them had clearly done so and fucked off.

When someone tapped his shoulder, Rhys' pulse spiked, and he spun around with his fists raised. Tears still blurred his sight and stung his eyes. It took several blinks before he trusted his vision. "Vicky?" Before she could respond, he said, "I thought you were dead."

She laughed and handed him his bat. "What made you think that?"

Rhys pointed at the florist's. "There's a dead body in the shop. About your height and build; it even has your hair."

"Oh shit," Vicky said as she clamped a hand over her mouth, "you thought that was me? I'm sorry; that was the florist. She was trapped inside her shop when I busted in. Two diseased followed me under the shutter and attacked her first. It gave me the time to find a weapon." Her body slumped as she looked down and sighed. "She didn't stand a chance. After I killed them, I had to take the florist out too."

When his vision cleared, Rhys looked at the patches of blood all over Vicky's clothes. Two brown stains as big as pizzas sat on either thigh.

The tears came back, so Rhys wiped his face. "Look at me, I'm a bloody mess. Sorry, it's been a long day."

Vicky took one of his hands. "I'm fine, honey, you don't need to worry anymore. I watched you lead the diseased into the other building from the roof of the florist's. By the time you'd jumped across, most of them had followed you inside. It was the perfect opportunity for me to get the fuck out of there. I had no way of telling you that, sorry."

Rhys moved forward and wrapped her in a tight hug. He squeezed so hard she made a fake choking noise. "It's okay. You're alive, that's all that matters."

As he pulled away, he kissed her cheek. Despite the blood all over her, she still smelled of her perfume, a fresh floral mix that reminded him of a summer breeze.

Without a word between them, the pair stared at one another, their faces close. Rhys' heart beat hard.

When Vicky leaned forwards, Rhys didn't need any more of an excuse.

The kiss stimulated a spike of adrenaline. After a day of anxiety, euphoria rushed through him. Everything else vanished at that moment, and it left just them in the world. For the briefest of seconds, there were no diseased, no death, no fear.

When they broke apart, the sweet taste of Vicky remained on Rhys' lips.

Vicky smiled. "Thank you for saving me."

Rhys held her waist and smiled back. "I had to pay you back for all you've done for me." His cheeks burned. "With rescuing you I mean—not the kiss. That wasn't paying you back. Oh, god, shall I just shut up now?"

Vicky laughed. "Come on, lover-boy; we have a six year old who needs our help."

A quick nod, and he pulled away from Vicky. When he leaned over the side of the bridge, he saw past the raised section and had a clear view of the drawbridge's control tower. He waved his arms in the air so those in the control box could see him. They had time to lower it and let them across before the diseased twigged.

But the bridge didn't move.

Rhys tried again and jumped up and down as he waved his arms.

Still nothing.

"What the fuck?"

Vicky moved to his side. "What are you trying to do?"

"I need the officer on the other side to lower the bridge so we can get across."

After she'd leaned forward, Vicky squinted and looked across the bridge. "There's no one in the booth."

"What?" Rhys looked again, his eyesight evidently not as good as hers. It didn't help that the windows of the booth were filthy. "You sure?"

"Positive."

Rhys looked up at the overcrowded roof of the first tower and then down at the wide river. The answer to his question stared back at him, yet he asked it anyway. "What are we going to do now?"

Chapter Thirty-Seven

The pair moved a few steps down the riverbank on the side of the bridge farthest away from the tower with the diseased on top. They crouched down out of their view.

A violent shake ran through Rhys' legs as he squatted next to Vicky. It made him look more scared than he felt, although not by much. "The river's the only way across," he said as he searched their surroundings. No more than a grassy hill, the riverbank left few places for the diseased to hide. "But the current's too rough for us to swim. There must be somewhere we can get…"—then he saw it—"Look, Vicky, there's a row boat down there. It's been dragged onto the riverbank. How hard can it be to get it back into the water?"

After she'd looked at the boat, Vicky nodded. "Okay, let's do it. I want off this goddamned island and the diseased can't swim, so it makes sense."

A quick peek over the wall, and Rhys saw that the diseased on the roof hadn't noticed them yet. They still reached across the gap. They still roared and screamed. They still fell from the edge like lemmings.

"Come on," he said, "they haven't twigged yet, let's go." With that, he started his descent down the riverbank to the abandoned boat.

As Rhys ran, he checked behind in case something followed them over. He saw trees along the pavement, parked cars, and the tops of the food pods. The diseased could come from anywhere. He glanced at the tower again; they still hadn't seen them.

They travelled so far down the bank that they couldn't see the diseased on the tower anymore, even though the air remained alive with their furious calls.

As they got closer to the boat, new sounds competed with the groans of the diseased: the sound of lapping water and their footsteps as they squelched over the soft ground. It never truly banished the background hum of the diseased that ran as an undercurrent of horror and served as a potent reminder that they were never safe. It almost dared them to drop their guard, to relax and take their safety for granted... to think they had the monsters beat, but the second they did, the diseased would be on their backs.

When Rhys turned to look at Vicky behind him, his entire world rocked as if he'd just taken a blow to the face. His legs buckled and he reeled for a second. He stared at it, and it stared straight back. Of all the places he'd looked before they began their descent, and he hadn't fucking looked there.

He'd dropped his guard already.

Chapter Thirty-Eight

Rhys stopped and maintained eye contact with the diseased beneath the bridge. Hidden half in shadow, he saw just one of its bloody eyes. It stared straight at him with the detached fury of a mass murderer ready to strike.

With his bat raised, Rhys ran at the monster. His feet sank into the soft ground. It sapped both his speed and strength. Had the way been flat and dry, he would have made it in time. Instead, he watched the thing's chest expand as it inhaled.

Rhys wanted to yell for it to stop—as though that would do any good.

Its scream came out as a primal braying call to anyone and everyone around them. When Rhys turned to Vicky, he saw her wide eyes and slack jaw as she stood there dumbstruck. "Go and start on the boat, now! I'll catch up."

She took off again in the direction of the boat.

Now that he'd travelled higher up the hill, Rhys could see the undeveloped tower again. Despite the distance, he felt like he could see every pair of bloody eyes as the entire rooftop of diseased looked his way.

The one beneath the bridge screamed again. Those on the roof replied in kind and a cacophony of chaos answered the song of one of their own. One check beneath the bridge and a swing of his bat could have prevented this.

The one beneath the bridge then ran at Rhys. It moved over the muddy ground with ease and picked up its pace. Rhys had just one chance to take it down, as it was both quicker and stronger than he was. With his sweaty grip clenched around the bat's handle, he pulled it back and swung.

The bat pinged as it connected with the thing's jaw. The vibration ran through the handle and up Rhys' arm. The creature stumbled and fell backwards.

In two strides, Rhys stood over it, his bat raised again.

Another heavy swing, and the thing's head caved in with a wet squelch. Rhys spat on it. "Fucker!"

After a moment's pause, Rhys heard it. Hundreds of clumsy feet played a tattoo against the ground. He heard a thousand screams. Bloodlust rushed at him like a tsunami.

If only he'd looked under the bridge before he ran toward the boat. *What a fucking idiot!*

Chapter Thirty-Nine

Vicky had made it to the boat and Rhys ran toward her as fast as he could. "Hurry up, Vick."

Although she pulled on the front of the vessel, it didn't budge. When she looked up, her face glowed red from the effort.

The screams from the group of diseased grew louder. Their feet shook the ground like an earthquake.

When Rhys got to the boat, he threw his bat in, grabbed the side, and pulled.

Nothing. The mud held it like super glue.

"Right," Rhys said. "We need to work together. One, two, three, pull."

They both yanked the boat backwards. It shifted by about an inch.

"Good; one, two, three, pull."

It came back a little farther.

"Pull."

"Pull."

Each tug moved the boat closer to the water's edge. As he pulled, Rhys looked up the riverbank. The diseased hadn't arrived yet, but the stampede grew louder. After he'd seen how the one beneath the bridge moved, he knew the muddy ground wouldn't slow them down one bit.

Another yank, and Rhys lost his grip on the edge of the boat. He slipped and landed in the wet mud with a *squelch*.

Damp earth turned his hands slick when he pushed himself up again. A quick rub against his trouser legs barely removed any of it.

He grabbed the boat and tugged so hard his body snapped back with every jerk. "Pull, pull, pull, pull." It started to move.

With the boat just a few metres from the water, Rhys looked up. The front-runners appeared at the top of the hill. Crusted blood streaked their cheeks, and their mouths hung open as dark holes. No more than fifty metres separated them. Pure hate drove them on.

"Pull, pull, pull, pull."

The boat moved some more and resisted less when they got to the wetter mud by the river. The calls of rage rushed toward them in a tide, and Rhys heard Vicky's panicked breath.

He looked across to see her slow down. "Keep pulling, Vick. Don't give up now."

More diseased came over the ridge and rushed at them. The front-runners were no more than twenty metres away.

The boat came free and slid into the water with a splash.

Rhys ran into the cold river and dragged it out with him. "Get in."

As Vicky jumped in and set the oars up, Rhys continued to drag the boat out.

The water came up to Rhys' thighs by the time Vicky had

clicked the second oar into place. Rhys pulled himself up into the boat, retrieved his bat, and moved to the side closest to the oncoming horde.

The front-runners splashed into the water. It slowed them down a little, but not enough to make much of a difference.

Rhys pulled his bat back and swung at the lead diseased.

He connected with a *ching* and it went down instantly. The ones behind trampled it as it disappeared beneath the water.

One grabbed the boat and Rhys swung at it. Then another. Then another.

Each swing connected. "Are you sure they can't swim?" Rhys called over his shoulder, and then swung for another one of the diseased.

"No."

"*What?*" Rhys took another one down.

"I said no. I'm not sure. It's just what I was told."

"Fuck." Another one fell beneath the water. "Why didn't you say?"

The effort of rowing delayed Vicky's reply. "Because it wouldn't have made any difference; we had to get in the boat. We had no other choice."

Yet another downed diseased, and Rhys wound back for another swing. However, as the gap between the boat and the shoreline increased, the diseased started to sink. They continued to rush forward, but they hit the point where the water level had risen to their neck and they went under.

They flailed their arms and gasped as their heads disappeared beneath the surface, but they never came back up again.

Diseased after diseased ran to their violent end and Rhys

watched them, his bat still ready to swing.

In the space of about thirty seconds, what could have been tens—maybe even a hundred—of the stupid bastards had vanished.

The rest finally stopped. They stood in the waist-deep water and watched Rhys and Vicky pull farther away from them. Still they reached out, they grasped at the air, they snapped their jaws, they screamed, but none of them advanced.

It was the roof of the abandoned building and car park all over again. The gap between them may have been small, but for the diseased, it might as well have been a mile. They stood and stared. They growled and hissed. They directed their collective attention and hate at the pair on the boat, but they'd been immobilised by a few feet of water.

While he fought to get his breath back, Rhys laughed. "They can't swim, Vicky." He turned to see her red-faced and panting. He laughed again. "They can't swim."

Vicky peered over his shoulder at the diseased on the shore. With a weary sigh, she slumped forward and let the boat continue to drift away from the mob.

Chapter Forty

"Let me row," Rhys said. "You've done enough already."

The boat drifted as Vicky looked up from her slumped position. "You sure?"

A quick nod and Rhys shifted over to the side so they could swap places. As they moved around in the small boat, they brushed up against one another. When Rhys looked into Vicky's eyes, the memory of their kiss flooded back and he could almost taste it again. Heat spread across his face, and he looked away.

Once they'd switched sides, Rhys stared to row. With his back to their direction of travel, he now watched the diseased on the riverbank. More came over the top all the time. They shoved those at the front forward as they had on the towers. It pushed more of the horrible creatures into the water. They gasped and flailed for a few seconds before they sank out of sight. "I would have thought the diseased could survive underwater."

After a check over her shoulder, Vicky turned back to Rhys. "They're not dead, just infected. They smell like they're dead, but they need to breathe just like you or I. It seems that the virus takes away the control of their limbs, so they can't swim. You've seen how the clumsy fuckers run. No wonder they can't cope with the water."

"Thank god!" Rhys said. At least two hundred faces stared at him. They snapped their jaws and bit at the air as if it would give them a taste of their prey. "Imagine if those fuckers could get across the water too."

With clenched teeth, Rhys dug deep and pulled the oars against the resistance of the water. He then took his attention away from the diseased on the riverbank and looked at Vicky instead. "So that's why this place is surrounded by a moat. I always wondered how it would stop people getting in, but it isn't to prevent people getting in, is it? It's about keeping the diseased contained. If it all went to shit, they could lock the place down, quarantine it, and keep the rest of the country safe. Blow the bridges, close the buildings off, and raise the drawbridge. Virus contained! Simple!"

After she'd turned to look over her shoulder again, Vicky said, "You're right, I don't know why I didn't see it before. It's so damn obvious now. I bet when the virus made it to the final stages of testing, they watched The Alpha Tower night and day. With something so contagious, the risk of it getting out had to be high. Maybe they didn't see a terrorist attack coming, but you can be damn sure someone was watching, ready to throw the city into lockdown when the diseased emerged."

"Well, that's a good thing for Flynn, at least," Rhys said. "The police barricade shows that the diseased failed to get across the water."

The slightest smile twitched on Vicky's lips. It vanished after she'd looked at the city behind them again. "I'm just glad I'm not locked in one of those buildings."

Rhys looked at the now metal-encased towers that made up Summit City's skyline. A deep sigh and he shook his head. "How the fuck will Dave get out?"

***

The screams of the diseased and the wild splashing as those at the front drowned got quieter the farther Rhys and Vicky got away from them. Rhys focused on the oars as they beat a steady retreat against the water, and the diseased calls became no more than a background noise.

When Vicky sat up straight, the wind tossed her hair. Rhys admired her for a second. When she looked back at him, his cheeks flushed and he cleared his throat. "I was... uh, I was worried about you, you know? Petrified, in fact, when I saw you run toward the florist's. There was no way I could have left you. Ever."

Vicky smiled as she looked at him. Her hair still danced on the wind. She then leaned forward and put a hand on his knee.

Rhys lifted the oars into the boat then held the back of her hand and gave it a gentle squeeze, his hand still dirty from the fall into the mud. He then resumed rowing.

***

With only a quarter of their journey left, Vicky insisted they swap around again so she could row the last bit. Rhys protested at first but he gave in quickly. God knows the burning muscles in his back appreciated the rest.

As Vicky ploughed on, Rhys removed the photo of Flynn

and the lump of painted and varnished wood from his pocket. The water had gotten to both, although the image on the photo remained in good condition. When Rhys spoke, his voice trembled. "Flynn's okay, isn't he?"

When Vicky didn't respond, Rhys looked up. She stared at him with a soft gaze and tight lips. She didn't know. How could she? Until they reached the other side, they couldn't know anything.

After the silence had hung between them for a few seconds, she said, "If the police barricade is anything to go by, I think he'll be fine. They hadn't been bitten."

With a weary sigh, Rhys put the photo back into his pocket. He stared past Vicky at the riverbank. Only time would tell.

***

Just before they reached the other side of the river, Rhys said, "Oh, I forgot to tell you. I saw something strange when I was in the towers next to the florist."

"Stranger than an army of enraged lunatics wanting to bite your face off?"

Rhys laughed. "Fair point. It was how they behaved. Up until that moment, I knew they communicated with one another, but I didn't realise they felt empathy for each other too."

"How do you know that?"

"They caught up with me at the top of the stairs and I hit the lead one in the face with a sledgehammer. He fell back into the others, who caught him and then held him to check he was okay. I didn't think it was possible, but when they realised he wasn't, it incensed them further. They wanted my blood more than before."

Vicky's eyes widened. "That sounds petrifying."

"It wasn't pretty. It makes me wonder what they're capable of. Can they communicate beyond that strange hunting call we've heard? Will they evolve into something far more deadly than we can fight? I mean, if those things were even half-intelligent, we wouldn't have got out of the city. What if they're capable of better organisation than they currently have? They'll be unstoppable."

Another glance at the collection of diseased on the riverbank made Rhys shiver. The width of the river had given him comfort but now they'd reached the other side, the expanse of water seemed like a pitiful defence. Surely, the diseased would find a way across.

Chapter Forty-One

Still soaked from where he'd dragged the boat out on the other side of the river, Rhys plunged into the frigid water again. A couple of kicks and his tiptoes found the soft riverbed. He pushed forward and dragged the boat with him until he had a solid footing. It made it much easier to pull it to the shore.

The bottom of the vessel bit into the soft mud. After another tug to be sure it was secure, Rhys held his hand out to Vicky. Not that she needed to, but she took it just the same. She held both baseball bats and the rope to tether the boat in her other hand.

After Vicky had tied the boat up, the pair climbed the steep incline to the road.

At the top, Rhys chewed on his bottom lip and looked both ways. "Where is everyone? This ain't right."

"You're telling me," Vicky said.

"I understand they may have quarantined the place, but no police?"

Vicky walked past him in the direction of the control booth for the bridge.

The sound of insatiable hunger rode across the river from the horde on the other side. The distance that separated them muted their enraged calls. With his nerves on edge, Rhys ignored the monsters and looked at the area that had been abandoned by the police. "Where have they gone?"

Vicky didn't answer him.

The control booth could fit two people, but it would be a squeeze. Rhys decided to wait outside—better not invade Vicky's personal space too much.

Between checks over his shoulder and across the river, Rhys watched Vicky remove her card, slide it into the card reader, and tap away at the keyboard.

The stillness closed in around Rhys, and his eyes stung from where he'd sweated into them all day. With his bat still raised, he looked and listened for signs of trouble.

Aside from the cries from the other side of the river, he saw and heard nothing—not even birdsongs.

When Vicky called out, Rhys jumped.

"Rhys, look at this."

After one last check up and down the road, Rhys stepped into the booth. It felt like he'd entered a greenhouse. The large windows elevated the temperature to what felt like a thousand degrees. Rhys moved his elbows away from his body to let his armpits breathe, but it did little to stop the itch and then trickle of sweat that ran down his sides. The air held a stagnant funk of coffee and dirt. "How the fuck does anyone spend time in this place?"

Instead of a response to his question, Vicky tapped the screen and brought up a countdown clock. It read six hours and twenty-three minutes.

"What's it for?" Rhys asked.

"It's how long that's left before they incinerate the island."

"Incinerate?"

Vicky nodded.

"But what about all of the people not infected? What about all of those locked in the buildings? How will they get out?"

A frown wrinkled Vicky's brow. "I think those in power would argue that the needs of the many outnumber the needs of the few. They certainly have in the past." She pointed out of the window. "Whatever happens, the virus can't cross that river."

"What about Dave? What about Larissa? Sure, she's a bitch, but she's still the mother of my child. There must be a way to stop it?"

"There is."

Her tone said it all. "I don't want to hear what it is, do I?"

Vicky shrugged, "The place to override it is in a small office in The Alpha Tower. The office itself is a nightmare to get into. It's high security shit. To be honest, if someone can get in there, then they deserve to be saved."

Rhys scoffed. "They probably deserve to die more than anyone. They created the virus."

"It was only a select few in The Alpha Tower who were responsible for this mess." There was an injured tone to her voice.

"I'm sorry, Vicky, I didn't mean—"

She showed him the palm of her hand. "It's fine."

"It's just, if they have security clearance, the chances are they were one of the few responsible for this fucking mess."

The heat in the booth seemed to rise, and Rhys fanned himself with his shirt. "Anyway, I ain't going back over that river for shit. I just want to get my son and get the fuck out of here."

"I don't blame you," Vicky said. "And six hours is plenty of time to get far enough away. Are you ready to go?"

Rhys nodded.

***

Rhys peered through the window of the squad car on the side of the road and laughed. "I don't believe it, Vick. They left the keys in here."

When Rhys opened the door, heat rushed out of the car like it would a hot oven. It carried the smell of stale sweat and sugar. Rhys got in and started the engine. He then wound the window down and called to Vicky, "Come on then, slow coach."

"Me, slow? I've seen you run, remember?"

Rhys didn't respond as Vicky got into the passenger seat, slammed the door, scrunched her nose up at what he could only assume was the smell, and wound the window down.

Rhys said, "Buckle up then."

Vicky rolled her eyes, "All right, *Dad*."

When the belt clicked into place, Rhys shoved the car into gear and sped off.

***

As soon as they rounded the first corner, Rhys hit the brakes.

Vicky leaned forward in her seat. "What the fuck?"

Another police car sat on the side of the road on fire. The flames reached at least two metres into the air. The bodies of police officers littered the ground around it, all with their hands tied behind their backs, all with bullet holes through their foreheads.

"They're dead," Rhys said.

"Uh huh."

"Someone's killed them."

"Uh huh."

"But who?"

Although he didn't look across at her, he could feel Vicky's eyes on him. "It's just a guess, but I would say it's the same people responsible for releasing the virus in the first place."

"The East?"

"I would assume so."

"But how did they get the guns to do it?"

"Who knows," Vicky said, "but they did, and they have, so there's no point in dwelling on it."

A shake of his head, and Rhys pulled away.

As he steered through the carnage, he crossed his chest as if he had a god to pray to. "I don't know what the fuck's happening, but we need to get to Flynn now." Once he was through the mess, he put his foot down. The sharp acceleration threw him back in his seat as it kicked up loose stones from the road.

Chapter Forty-Two

Rhys slowed the car down again. Just a few minutes had passed since they'd left the aftermath of the mass police execution. He felt Vicky look across at him but kept his focus on the side of the road.

"What is it?" Vicky said.

The words had abandoned him. Instead, Rhys pointed at a house across the street, and more specifically, its white garage door.

Vicky drew a sharp breath and spoke as she exhaled. "Fuck."

As Rhys continued to look at the diagonal line of blood streaked up the garage door, he noticed the handprints next to it. They were subtle, but there nonetheless. He then looked at the driveway; the grey concrete was stained with yet more blood. His body and his voice shook as he said, "It's got out of the city. We've got to hurry." He revved the engine and spun away.

"But how?" Vicky said as they tore along the road. "The police were blatantly killed with bullets, not by the diseased."

The engine screamed as Rhys pushed the car to its limit through the empty streets. Although he kept his eyes on the road, he caught the flashes of red on front doors, driveways, and even cars. Blood coated the large front window of what appeared to be the only shop in town. Claret pooled on the pavement outside.

The tyres screeched as Rhys threw the car into the next bend, and he saw Vicky reach up and hold on to the handle above her head.

"Maybe the terrorists set them loose," Vicky said. "Killed the police and then let some out. They seem set on turning the virus against us."

Rhys' pulse pounded in his head as he swerved through a tight chicane. He gnawed on his bottom lip and his knuckles hurt from where he gripped the steering wheel so hard.

It didn't matter how far or fast they went, the virus had a lead on them. Rhys glanced at the pavement and said, "There's still blood on the streets, and we're only about five minutes away from Flynn's school."

Vicky didn't respond, but even with the chaos that raged through his mind, Rhys heard her whimper.

***

Before he'd even got to the school, Rhys' stomach turned backflips. "What if they're already there, Vicky? What if we're too late?"

"Let's just get there first. We can't do anything until we know what we're dealing with."

The second he saw the school gates, Rhys' chest constricted and the word came out as a wheeze. "No."

Vicky didn't speak.

Rhys skidded to a halt outside the school playground and stared through the bars. "No." He punched the steering wheel. "No!"

Pain, confusion, and anger stared back at him from the other side of the fence. Where there had once been joy as children played, there was now only torment and blood—lots of blood.

Tears stung Rhys' eyes and he shook his head. "We're too late." He gripped the steering wheel and shook it so hard the car rocked. "How has this fucking happened? My boy's in there. How did the virus get out of the city?"

Heavy sobs snapped through Rhys as he leaned over the wheel. He felt Vicky's arm across his shoulders and listened to her soft voice. "I'm so sorry, Rhys. I'm so, so sorry."

Sorry didn't make any difference to him. Rhys lifted his head. When he looked through the school's windows, he saw splashes of blood thrown up against nearly every one of them. The front door had been busted clean off its hinges and lay on the floor. What little he could see inside showed him pure carnage, like a tornado of razor blades had torn through the building.

While he rocked in his seat, Rhys shook his head. "No, no, this can't be happening. No."

A deep breath, and he sat up straight then leaned into the back of the car and pulled his bat off the seat.

"Don't get out of the car, Rhys," Vicky said.

Although he'd heard her, Rhys popped the door open. The stupid and agonised groans of the diseased grew louder. They moaned and writhed as if in perpetual pain. Hopefully they were; the nasty things that had taken his son deserved nothing but utter torment.

At first, the diseased simply watched him. They seemed to understand that bars separated them, although they hadn't worked out that all they had to do was find the open gate and walk through it. As he got closer to the fence, the diseased in the playground moved forward and pressed themselves against the bars.

Rhys stood still and watched the ones at the front. The thick metal pushed into their flesh as they had pressure applied from the second wave behind them. It pulled at their skin and turned their already gruesome masks of disease into something more twisted and inhuman than they already were. Instead of reaching forward with their hands, the monsters bit at the air. They needed to taste him.

Heavy breaths on Rhys' left broke him from his trance. He turned in time to see an infected woman. She ran directly at him, her mouth open wide as blood flowed down her chin. Because of her short sleeves, Rhys saw the bite mark on her arm. No two people were turned in the same way. The diseased seemed to attack whatever part of the body they could get to.

Tears blurred Rhys' vision, but he could see enough. Rhys yelled out and put everything he had into his swing.

The bat and her head connected with a *ping*, and the vibration ran a momentary ache directly to his elbows.

She dropped to the floor as her legs gave up mid-stride.

Before he could make sure with another blow to the head, a second diseased rounded the corner. This one was a man—the headmaster of the school, no less.

This time, Rhys ran at him. "Why didn't you save them? You should have done more, you useless fuck!"

The headmaster screamed no differently than the other diseased.

Rhys screamed back and swung.

The headmaster fell.

When Rhys heard the slam of another car door, he turned to see Vicky. He pointed at her and his voice cracked as he shouted, "Get back in the car, now."

With her bat in her hand, she shook her head. "No. Not if you won't. I'm not letting you go down like this. And if you go, I'm going down with you."

More footsteps approached them.

A little boy came at Rhys fast. Being about the same build as Flynn, Rhys' heart stopped as he stared at him—but it wasn't Flynn. It looked nothing like him, in fact. If Rhys had more involvement in his boy's life, he would probably be able to name the kid as one of Flynn's classmates. He would have probably seen him at the various kids' parties that he would have attended, but he didn't. A part-time dad didn't hold that kind of information, and he wasn't even that; he'd been demoted to a photo in Flynn's room, at best.

Reluctance weakened his muscles as he stared at the boy, but he had to do it. The kid had gone. The kid had gone like Flynn had gone. A monster remained. A monster that could only create more monsters.

The kid's skull gave more easily than those of the adults before him. It felt like swinging at an egg.

The broken form of the little boy crashed to the floor, his limbs splayed; his dark mouth wide. Tears ran down Rhys' cheeks as he stared at the small and broken body. A frozen look of horror stretched across his tiny face.

More diseased burst from the school; Rhys shook as he lifted his bat and swallowed back the lump in his throat. The people who had once occupied the bodies had long since left. Men, women, children; it didn't matter anymore. The same monster stared at him from every set of bleeding eyes. The same hive mind hell bent on the eradication of the human race.

As they got close, Rhys yelled, stepped forward, and swung his bat.

Chapter Forty-Three

Rhys lost the use of his arms when one of them grabbed him from behind in a bear hug. What an idiot! With his emotions so high, he'd not even thought to watch his back.

Sharp twists and turns did nothing to help him break free from the vice-like grip.

As he stood there, helpless and restrained, Rhys flinched in anticipation of the huge bite about to bury into his neck until a voice found a way through his fury.

"Rhys, it's me. You need to get your head together and get back in the car." When Vicky let him go, she tugged on his arm. "Come on, we need to get out of here."

A continuous stream of diseased exited the school and filled the playground. If they stayed, they'd die. Vicky was right; they couldn't fight them all.

As Rhys followed Vicky to the car, he headed for the passenger seat. Several checks behind, and he watched the playground fill up with the monsters.

When he got in, he slammed the door and locked it. Despite the fact that some of the diseased had come through the gate, most of them seemed yet to find it and remained constrained by the fence between the car and the playground. "I just need to know what's happened to him," Rhys said. "Either way, I need to know."

Before Vicky could respond, three more diseased found their way out. They screamed and yelled as they headed straight for the squad car.

Vicky slammed the car into reverse and the engine roared as the vehicle jerked backwards.

While Vicky looked out of the back window, Rhys stared out of the front. He watched the three give chase. "The fuckers look like they can barely stand up. How can they run so fast?"

Vicky slammed the brake on, which locked the wheels and spun the car one hundred and eighty degrees. A lurch of nausea surged through Rhys.

She then threw it into first and accelerated away, her blue eyes hooded by a scowl as she checked the rear-view mirror. With her attention divided between the road ahead and the beasts behind, she said, "How the fuck did the virus get out of Summit City? How did it travel so fast? The terrorists must have let it out. I can't think of any other explanation."

A weary sigh and Rhys sank deeper into his seat. He watched the world flash past. A world without his son. He found it hard to give a fuck about anything else. "I don't know, Vicky, but I'm guessing we're fucked now it's out. The river was our best hope of containing it. Because that hasn't happened, we're screwed." A deep ache ran through his heart and his eyes watered. "I've failed my boy. The one thing I needed to do when everything turned to shit and I've fucked it up."

The picture of Flynn remained in his shirt's top pocket. Rhys pulled it out and stared at it. A sharp lump clawed its way up his throat and dug its nails in.

Another check in the rear-view mirror then Vicky dropped a hand on Rhys' shoulder. She gave it a gentle squeeze before she grabbed the wheel again.

Rhys took the bark from his trouser pocket and stroked the varnished surface. His hands knew every bump of the gift, and his fingers ran familiar paths through its waxed peaks and valleys. "This world seems pointless without Flynn."

Before Vicky could reply, Rhys sat bolt upright and turned to her. "We have to go back."

"What? Are you fucking kidding me?"

He lifted the bark and waved it at her. "No, I'm not. Very far from it." Heavy breaths rocked him where he sat. "Flynn might still be alive."

Chapter Forty-Four

Vicky drove back with the same determination she'd escaped with, and Rhys had to hold the handle above the window to keep himself steady. Fear, excitement, and motion sickness wrestled for control of his guts. His palms turned slick with sweat.

He swallowed the hot saliva that rained down his throat and said, "The park is just next to the school. Why didn't I think of it first? Flynn loves to climb; especially in the park." He held the bark up. "It's where he got this from. He told me about it; he climbed as high as he could up the tree and pulled it off. That was a few years back, so I'm sure he can climb much higher now. By the time he leaves primary school, he said he wants to be able to climb so high he can catch the clouds."

"And you think he managed to get out and make it up there?"

The words hit Rhys like a gut punch and momentarily silenced him. His assertion of a few seconds ago wavered. "I can only hope, Vicky, and as long as I have hope it's worth going back."

"But what if he isn't there?"

For a moment, Rhys couldn't find the words. He stared at Vicky and ground his jaw. A deep breath released some of his tension. "I know what you're trying to do, and I know you think it's the right thing."

Vicky raised an eyebrow.

"You're trying to get me familiar with the idea that Flynn's dead. That's how we work, isn't it? Humans, I mean. We set ourselves up for the worse possible scenario so we don't get our hopes up. We try to feel despair before we know whether we need to or not. First of all, how can I prepare myself for the realisation that my boy's dead? No amount of thinking it will make me any less devastated if it's true. I can't synthesise those feelings before they come to me. Secondly, it's my boy. If there's any chance he's still alive—and until I see his corpse, or him under the twitching and bleeding effect of this virus, then there is a chance—I'm going to hang on to hope. It's all I have. I'm not giving up until I have to."

As the pair shot past the front of the school, Rhys pointed at the park next to it. "It's there; that huge tree in the middle."

A mob of about twenty diseased had gathered around the foot of the large oak tree. As one, they clawed and grabbed at its trunk. Their inability to climb it showed in their frustrated and pathetic attempts to reach up into the branches. The group only had four or five adults in it. All of the others were children.

Rhys squinted as he looked at the crowd. "Flynn isn't in that mob."

"How can you tell?"

It was a fair question. Not only were they quite far away, but the virus added an alien element to its host. The concentrated fury of it turned them into a darker and more horrific version of themselves. Some of them didn't even look like people anymore. But it didn't matter how twisted the creatures were; Rhys would know if his boy was there. "I just know."

Vicky didn't respond.

The summer heat had cooked the car up, and sweat ran from Rhys' armpits down his side. Better that than open the windows though. On a normal drive, Rhys would have worked out the air conditioning by now. Instead, he leaned forward and stared into the tree. The thick leaves made it hard to see if anyone was up it.

"Something's got them riled up," Rhys said. "I need you to drive into the park so we can get a better look."

Vicky's immediate compliance sent a loud *clunk* through the car when she drove over the curb and onto the grass.

"Are you trying to get a flat?" Rhys said.

Vicky ignored him as she sped across the bumpy ground. The car jumped around like a bean on a bass speaker.

Rhys stared into the tree. Because he wasn't looking, when they hit the first diseased kid, the loud *bang* made him jump.

As they got closer, Rhys saw something and hope swelled in his chest. It was a small and exposed leg in a pair of shorts. Then he saw a white polo shirt similar to the ones worn by the diseased children that surrounded the base of the tree. Then finally, he saw the wide eyes and pale face of a boy. Of his boy.

Grief rushed forward. It nearly both blinded and gagged him. After he'd cleared his throat, Rhys rubbed his eyes. "It's him, Vicky." Tears dampened his cheeks and he shook when he said, "It's Flynn."

Chapter Forty-Five

With the diseased so intent on Flynn up the tree, none of them bothered with the car as it drove past.

Rhys watched them as Vicky drove over to the corner of the park and turned around. Vicky's impatience manifested when she tapped the steering wheel. "What are we going to do now, Rhys?"

"Is twenty of them too many for us to fight?" he asked. "They're mostly kids."

Vicky stopped tapping and looked at him.

"I'll take that as a yes."

"Look," Vicky said, "I'll do it as a last resort. He's your boy, and we'll get him out of this situation one way or another. Although, I'd rather not go toe to toe with over twenty of them if I can avoid it; who knows how many more will come if we start a fight."

Out of the corner of his eye, Rhys saw a diseased by itself. When he looked at it, he gasped. "A baby."

"What?"

Rhys pointed at the diseased woman. "Look, that one over

there has a baby. It's not interested in attacking anyone because it's looking after that thing. It's like what I saw in the tower. These monsters look out for one another."

As Vicky watched the diseased woman and baby, the colour drained from her face. "It's fucking tragic what's happened. Government paranoia turned this conflict into a pissing contest between scientists who have zero empathy. They see the entire world as an experiment without any regard for consequence. They don't care that they've torn families apart."

While Vicky talked, the plan formed in Rhys' mind. He kept it to himself; she wouldn't go for it if he gave her a choice. He grabbed his bat off the back seat. "Wait here."

Vicky raised an eyebrow at him.

Once outside the car, Rhys pushed the door closed as quietly as possible. He took steps toward the woman. They were diseased; they weren't real people anymore. If he saw them as real, he'd lose the fight. He needed to win for Flynn's sake.

When he got close to the mother, he readied his bat. The mother then turned and looked straight at him. With her dark and bloody eyes fixed on him, she worked her mouth up and down as if to stretch a cramp from her jaw. Then she snarled and hissed. A wounded dog backed into a corner, she just wanted him to stay away. Her tongue, covered in blood, poked forward like a reptile's, and she pulled her little one in tighter.

Rhys stopped and stared at her.

Then he pushed on again.

As he got closer, she pulled her baby in and turned her shoulder around the infant so she faced him side on. The thought of it robbed some of the strength from Rhys. Diseased or not, a mother and child stood before him. He knew he couldn't treat them with that compassion. They didn't deserve it and their human form probably wouldn't want it. Rhys would want to be taken down instantly in their situation.

She opened her mouth to hiss again, and Rhys swung for her.

Like a puppet having its strings cut, the mother went down and hit the ground hard. The strength of her grip abandoned her and she let go of the infected child. It rolled away from her dead body and fell on its back. Its limbs pistoned out in random directions, but the baby didn't cry.

The taste of bile rose onto the back of Rhys' tongue as he watched it.

He then leaned down, grabbed one of its chubby ankles, and lifted it from the ground. There may have only been a few teeth in its mouth, but from the way it snapped and bit at the air between them, the little shit knew exactly how to use them.

As Rhys approached the car with the thing at arm's length, Vicky stared at him, her face slack. She wound the window down. "What the fuck are you doing?"

"Don't confuse this thing for human. It's one of them, and it's them against us."

With a deep frown, Vicky looked from Rhys to the baby and back again.

"Look, I just need you to trust me, okay?"

Vicky continued to watch the baby.

"I'm going to get on the roof of the car and bang on it when I want you to move or stop. I need you to drive over to the tree, but much slower this time. You got that?"

She continued to watch the baby.

"I said, have you got that?"

Vicky gulped and nodded.

Chapter Forty-Six

The climb onto the roof proved much harder because of the baby. Its tiny bloody eyes glared hate at him. No matter how small the thing, it wanted to fuck him up. When he was finally up and on his feet, Rhys stamped on the roof. "Remember to drive slowly, Vicky."

Even at the slow pace, the car shook over the lumpy ground and it threatened to throw Rhys off. With his arms held out for balance, he watched the baby swing like a pendulum from his grip. Its little mouth snapped every time it got close to him.

As they approached the tree, the diseased at the bottom continued to focus on Flynn.

Rhys stamped on the top of the car again when they got close, and Vicky came to an abrupt stop.

Everything moved in slow motion. Rhys' foot caught beneath the blue strip light that sat on the top of the car, and he fell. He reached out to soften his landing, which brought the baby closer. The ravenous little demon swung so near to his face that the castanet *click* of its teeth snapped in Rhys' ear.

When Rhys hit the roof of the car, he rolled onto his back

and lifted the baby away from him. He kept it at arm's length. The fall had instilled a new vigour in the horrible thing. It writhed and snapped with more ferocity than before. So close to tasting blood, it seemingly couldn't bear it.

Rhys got to his feet again, and the baby chewed at the air between them. He turned to the diseased beneath the tree. "Oi, you horrible bastards, look at me. I have one of you now."

As one unit—one mind—the pack turned and stared at Rhys. The usual expressions of hate locked their faces, but they quickly vanished when they saw the baby. Concern wrinkled brows and their aggression vanished.

Rhys swung the baby back and forth. He felt like a cruel older brother holding his sister's doll hostage. The diseased's eyes followed it like dogs on a stick—that's all the baby was: an inanimate object to be used as a toy. This thing wasn't human and didn't deserve to be treated as such.

The strength drained from his body as if his muscles questioned his actions. The little thing was a monster—nothing more. Rhys took a deep breath and pushed through it. He then yelled and launched the small child.

Bloody eyes stared, dark mouths hung open, and then, as one, the diseased chased it.

Another stamp on the roof and Vicky pulled toward the tree.

The bright sun shone into Rhys' eyes, and he had to shield his vision to see when he looked up. "Flynn, it's me. Daddy. You need to come down now, mate, before they come back."

For a moment, Flynn stared at Rhys and shook his head.

"Come on, we can't hang around. We've got to get out of here, now."

Flynn shook his head again, but he didn't speak.

A glance to the side showed the diseased gathered around the baby. "If you don't jump now, you'll die. We'll all die. Come on, Flynn."

When his little boy lowered one of his legs, Rhys saw the shake that ran through it. His heart tensed when he saw the dark patch that had spread around his crotch from where he'd pissed himself.

"That's it, you're doing really well."

The small black plimsoll found a foothold as Flynn got closer to his dad. Some of the diseased looked their way. Rhys' heart raced, but he tried to keep his voice even. "You're doing well, Flynn, but we need to speed it up a little, mate."

Flynn bit his lip in concentration and sped up.

Then Rhys heard it and it ran shards of frigidity down his spine... the primitive call from a diseased. It turned his entire body to gooseflesh and his pulse ran away from him. "Jump!" he said. "Jump now, Flynn."

Flynn slipped from the tree and landed in Rhys'' arms just as the pack ran toward them.

With a hard stamp on the roof, Rhys shouted, "Go, go, go, go."

As the sound of a stampede rushed forward, Vicky revved the engine hard and Rhys dropped down so he and his boy were crouched on top of the car.

A couple of hands slapped at the boot as it shot away, but none got any closer than that.

As they moved over the bumpy ground of the park, Rhys pulled Flynn in tight. With his little boy in his arms, Rhys sobbed like he'd never sobbed before.

Chapter Forty-Seven

When Vicky stopped the car, Rhys pulled out of the protective hug he'd wrapped his boy in; a glance around made it seem clear to him. "Come on, mate, let's get in."

Flynn sat up and hugged himself. It did little to stop him from shivering.

Rhys rubbed his back before Flynn looked down at where he'd wet himself.

Rhys dismissed it with a wave of his hand. "Don't worry about that; Vicky won't care. We'll get you a change of clothes en route."

The screams of the diseased rang through the air behind them. They hadn't given up yet. After Rhys slipped off the roof, he held his arms out to Flynn. "Come on, we need to hurry this up."

The roof bent and popped as Flynn walked across it and jumped down.

The second they closed the back doors, Vicky hit the gas and they sped off.

***

Everything had worked out. Rhys had his boy and a new lady in his life—so what if it had taken the end of the world for a woman to be interested in him again?

They had to pass Summit City on their way to The Highlands, but it would be behind them soon and they'd be home free. When Flynn squirmed, Rhys relaxed his hug on him. It was hard to let go after he'd pined for his touch for so long.

Rhys placed a kiss on top of his boy's head and breathed in his smell. "I thought I'd lost you, mate. Then I held the piece of bark you'd painted and varnished for me, and I knew you were all right. I just knew it."

Still gripped with a violent shake, Flynn stared at Vicky in the front seat. A frown crushed his features. "Where's Mum?"

Silence filled the car and Rhys made eye contact with Vicky via the rear-view mirror.

Flynn looked from his dad to Vicky and back to his dad again. A reedy panic tightened his words. "Where's Mum? What's happened to her? Is she dead?"

"No, she's not dead," Rhys said. "She's, um, she's trapped."

"Trapped?"

For the second time in as many minutes, Rhys and Vicky stared at one another. There seemed to be no point lying; he was only six, but the rules of life had changed drastically. "Those people that were trying to get at you in the trees aren't people anymore."

"What do you mean?"

"They're…" how could he describe it?

"Zombies?" Flynn asked.

"How do you know about zombies?"

"Mummy lets me play *Call of Duty: Zombies*."

"She lets you…" Rhys stopped himself. "They're pretty much zombies, but a hell of a lot faster. They came from Summit City. There's a science lab called The Alpha Tower where they made the virus."

The confusion on Flynn's face inspired Rhys to get to the point. "When the virus broke out, I was outside. Everyone who was in work still, like Mummy, got locked in their buildings. Shutters blocked every window, and they're now trapped inside."

"Are they safe?"

"For the time being." He looked into his boy's dark eyes. No lies; Flynn deserved more than that. "The thing is, mate, I'm not sure she'll get out."

The sound of Flynn's rapid breaths tore at Rhys' heart. "But they have to let her out; she's my mum. You have to do something, Dad. Can you go and get her?" A sheen of tears glazed Flynn's eyes. "I want my mum."

A rock sat in Rhys' stomach when he looked at Vicky in the rear-view mirror again. She shook her head, "No fucking way!"

"Language!"

Vicky's gaze flicked to Flynn, and then back to Rhys again. "I'm sorry, but there ain't no way I'm going back in there. It's madness. Let's just go to The Highlands and sit this out."

"You said there's a way to override the order to incinerate, right?"

Vicky didn't respond.

"Does that mean there's a way to override the shutters on the buildings too?"

"Are you insane, Rhys? If you open up the buildings, there's no way you're getting out of that city. There'll be too many people getting infected."

"Maybe I could use the chaos to get out. I'll have a plan so I'll be one step ahead of everyone else. I know what to expect. You've already said I need to get to The Alpha Tower to open the shutters, so will you tell me exactly how I do it, Vicky?"

For a moment, Vicky didn't respond. After she'd looked out of the window to her right, she sighed. "You need to get into The Alpha Tower and get up to the top floor. There's a room up there with a computer in it where you can turn off the incinerator. There's another computer that will override the lockdown system. It's pretty simple. The hard part is getting in there. My card will get you into The Alpha Tower, but once you're in, you'll need a scientist's card to get to the last room. As far as I know, they've all been bitten. It's a tower full of diseased now, but if you can kill one in a lab coat, you may find a card. I think it's suicide though, Rhys."

When Rhys looked at Flynn, the light glistened off his tear-streaked cheeks. "Can you draw me a map of the inside of The Alpha Tower?"

"And what are we going to do with, Flynn? We can't take a boy in there with us."

"I'm not asking you to come with me."

"Good."

"I need you to keep Flynn safe."

"What?"

Rhys wiped the tears from Flynn's face. "I want you to drop me off, take Flynn, and come back for me half an hour before the city's supposed to get wiped out. I'll be waiting."

Vicky frowned in the rear-view mirror but didn't respond.

When Rhys touched her shoulder, she flinched. "I need to do this, Vicky. It's the right thing to do. I need to do everything I can to make sure my boy has his mum."

Still no reply.

"Please?"

"What if you're not back?"

"I'll be back."

"I'm not so sure about that."

"Trust me, Vicky, I'll be back. I promise."

The same darkness sat on her features, but something had changed. He had her; she was going to do it.

Chapter Forty-Eight

The creak of the handbrake cut through the silence after Vicky stopped the car by the drawbridge. Waves of nausea ran through Rhys as he looked over at Summit City. Panic fluttered in his chest. They had a police car, baseball bats, a full tank of petrol, and his little boy; yet he was going back into the bowels of hell. Nevertheless, it was the right thing to do, and whether Larissa was a bitch or not, he owed it to his boy.

Vicky held up a pen and piece of paper. "I'm going to draw exactly where you need to go in The Alpha Tower, okay?"

"Thank you." Rhys then took Flynn's hand and unlatched the watch on his wrist. "I need to take this, mate." It was a multi-coloured Lego watch with Superman on the strap. "I need to keep track of the time while I'm in there."

Flynn nodded but didn't speak.

One last hug and kiss on the top of his head, and Rhys opened the back door. "I love you, Flynn. I'll be back with Mummy soon, okay?"

Flynn stared at him and nodded again. The same glaze returned to his brown eyes, and he didn't look like he had the words in him. Did he want to ask Rhys to stay? It looked like it, but he undoubtedly wanted his mum alive more.

Rhys retrieved his baseball bat from the floor of the car and got out. "Now remember to do whatever Vicky says. She'll look after you, but be good for her."

Flynn nodded again.

With Vicky by his side, Rhys walked over to the control booth. En route, Vicky handed her card to Rhys. "That'll get you into The Alpha Tower, even if the shutters are up."

Once they'd reached the control booth, Rhys leaned inside and removed two walkie–talkies. The red power light showed when he turned them on. "I'd imagine these will have a good enough range if you're close by." He passed one to Vicky. "I'll have mine turned off most of the time and only use it when it's safe. You'll need to leave yours on for the entire time, okay?"

Vicky took the walkie–talkie and slipped it into her pocket.

Rhys looked across the river into the city. "The coast looks clear." A tremble shook both his words and his limbs.

Vicky obviously saw his doubt. "It's not too late to change your mind, you know."

"All I want is to go to The Highlands with you two, but I'll never be able to look my boy in the eyes again if I don't try to save Larissa."

A shimmer of sadness washed across Vicky's face. "Just don't get yourself killed, okay? I was starting to like you."

Rhys tugged her toward him and the pair kissed. He tasted her salty tears. After he'd pulled away, he cleared his throat and said, "With you and Flynn as my motivation, I can survive anything. I promise you, Vicky, I'm coming back."

Heavy breaths ran through Vicky as she held the map out for him. Her hand shook. "There are two identical rooms at the end of the corridor at the top of The Alpha Tower. The controls to shut everything down are in the room on the left."

"And the room on the right?"

"Nothing; it's currently empty."

Vicky then went into the control booth and tapped on the computer that controlled the bridge.

A loud click and then a whir, and the bridge slowly lowered.

As Rhys stood and stared at it, his heart beat to the point where it felt like it would explode. What the fuck was he doing?

***

Once the bridge had been fully lowered, Rhys scanned around again for signs of the diseased. Although there were none, he could smell rotten meat and vinegar on the light breeze.

One last look over his shoulder and he saw both Vicky and Flynn staring at him through glass; Vicky, the glass of the booth, and Flynn, the glass of the car's back window.

He then turned away from them and looked ahead. His tears returned with full force and his throat ached. Deep unease sat in his gut as if his intuition needed him to listen to it—it didn't matter, Rhys had to do this. After one final, deep breath, he stepped onto the bridge.

Ends.

Thank you for reading The Alpha Plague.

Support the Author

Dear reader, as an independent author I don't have the resources of a huge publisher. If you like my work and would like to see more from me in the future, there are two things you can do to help: leaving a review, and a word-of-mouth referral.

Releasing a book takes many hours and hundreds of dollars. I love to write, and would love to continue to do so. All I ask is that you leave an Amazon review. It shows other readers that you've enjoyed the book and will encourage them to give it a try too. The review can be just one sentence, or as long as you like.

***

For all of my other titles and my mailing list - go to
www.michaelrobertson.co.uk

About The Author

Michael Robertson has been a writer for many years and has had poetry and short stories published, most notably with HarperCollins. He first discovered his desire to write as a skinny weed-smoking seventeen-year-old badman who thought he could spit bars over drum and bass. Fortunately, that venture never left his best mate's bedroom and only a few people had to endure his musical embarrassment. He hasn't so much as looked at a microphone since. What the experience taught him was that he liked to write. So that's what he did.

After sending poetry to countless publications and receiving MANY rejection letters, he uttered the words, "That's it, I give up." The very next day, his first acceptance letter arrived in the post. He saw it as a sign that he would find his way in the world as a writer.

Over a decade and a half later, he now has a young family to inspire him and has decided to follow his joy with every ounce of his being. With the support of his amazing partner, Amy, he's managed to find the time to take the first step of what promises to be an incredible journey. Love, hope, and the need to eat get him out of bed every morning to spend a precious few hours pursuing his purpose.

If you want to connect with Michael:

Subscribe to my newsletter at –
www.michaelrobertson.co.uk

Email me at –
subscribers@michaelrobertson.co.uk

Follow me on Facebook at –
www.facebook.com/MichaelRobertsonAuthor

Twitter at –
@MicRobertson

Google Plus at –
plus.google.com/u/0/113009673177382863155/posts

DEAD ISLAND: *Operation Zulu*

Ten years after the world was nearly brought to its knees by a zombie Armageddon, there is a race for the antidote! On a remote Caribbean island, surrounded by a horde of hungry living dead, a team of American and Australian commandos must rescue the Antidotes' scientist. Filled with zombies, guns, Russian bad guys, shady government types, serial killers and elevator muzak. Dead Island is an action packed blood soaked horror adventure.

Allen Gamboa

INVASION OF THE DEAD SERIES

On the east coast of Australia, five friends returning from a month-long camping trip slowly discover that a virus has swept through much of the country. What greets them in a gradual revelation is an enemy beyond compare. Armed with dwindling ammunition, the friends must overcome their disagreements, utilize their individual skills, and face unimaginable horrors as they battle to reach their hometown and make sense of life in the new world.

Owen Baillie

SIXTH CYCLE
Nuclear war has destroyed human civilization.
Captain Jake Phillips wakes into a dangerous new world, where he finds the remaining fragments of the population living in a series of strongholds, connected across the country. Uneasy alliances have maintained their safety, but things are about to change. — **Discovery leads to danger.** — Skye Reed, a tracker from the Omega stronghold, uncovers a threat that could spell the end for their fragile society. With friends and enemies revealing truths about the past, she will need to decide who to trust. — **Sixth Cycle** is a gritty post-apocalyptic story of survival and adventure.
Darren Wearmouth ~ Carl Sinclair

SPLINTER
For close to a thousand years they waited, waited for the old knowledge to fade away into the mists of myth. They waited for a re-birth of the time of legend for the time when demons ruled and man was the fodder upon which they fed. They waited for the time when the old gods die and something new was anxious to take their place. **A young couple was all that stood between humanity and annihilation.** Ill equipped and shocked by the horrors thrust upon them they would fight in the only way they knew how, tooth and nail. Would they be enough to prevent the creation of the feasting hordes? Were they alone able to stand against evil banished from hell? **Would the horsemen ride when humanity failed?** The earth would rue the day a splinter group set up shop in Cold Spring.
H. J. Harry

WHISKEY TANGO FOXTROT SERIES
The world is at war with the Primal Virus. Military forces across the globe have been recalled to defend the homelands as the virus spreads and decimates populations. Out on patrol and assigned to a remote base in Afghanistan, Staff Sergeant Brad Thompson's unit was abandoned and left behind, alone and without contact. They survived and have built a refuge, but now they are forgotten. **No contact with their families or commands.** Brad makes a tough decision to leave the safety of his compound to try and make contact with the States, desperate to find rescue for his men. **What he finds is worse than he could have ever predicted.**
W. J. Lundy

<<<<>>>>

Printed in Great
Britain
by Amazon